Golden Iris

Golden Iris

By R. Poling

Alto Media

GOLDEN IRIS
Published by Alto Media LLC
2060 Highbluff Dr NE
Grand Rapids, MI 49505 U.S.A.

Alto Media and the graphic music note logo are registered trademarks of Alto Media LLC

ISBN
KDP Paperback 978-1-0815-9727-6

Cover Design: Olive Design @itsolivedesign
Author Photo: Ann-Marie Jurek, 2018

Special thanks to Janay Faulkner for her invaluable help in editing my Italian (and English)

Second Edition 2021

Language Note:

Words in English appear in Times New Roman

Words translated from Italian appear in Caveat

Le parole stampate in Italiano appaiono in corsivo
(Words printed in Italian appear in italic)

For all the unnamed policemen
taken down by the hero

1

In Italy, in April; on a Tuesday, early - *The Golden Flower* smelled like gunsmoke and blood. Flashing lights and loud sirens were quickly destroying the few remnants of beauty in the restaurant's atmosphere, now that the haunting piano music had stopped. If this had been a movie, the soundtrack would have carried the piano's melody over the muted sounds of the scene, and Tera, handcuffed, would have been escorted out of the building in slow motion by the Italian Military Police; some heavy lens flare effects applied to the spinning blue lights; dramatic close-ups on the police marshall's face, and Tera's tired eyes. But this wasn't a movie. It was very real, and Tera felt stunned, almost numb; awkwardly sitting at the piano, she could no longer continue to play.

For a good two seconds, she thought about running. But even in her current state of mental and physical exhaustion, she recognized that running would be a very bad idea. She took the money, though. Technically she earned it. Despite the environment of death that seemed to be following her around, Tera kept her focus. She scanned the room quickly. The man was already gone - didn't even stick around to hear his request. "Oh great..." she thought, "What have I gotten into?" After snatching the man's money from the edge of the piano and fitting it carefully down her black evening gown, she took a deep breath and tried to remain calm.

The men outside were calling to each other in Italian as they quickly swept around the building: dark figures casting shadows in the night as blinding blue spun relentlessly in dancing patterns. Mounted gun-lights whizzed around in all directions, dotting the windows with glares. She lifted her hands in the air, which triggered some reflex for a long and deep yawn. Even in shock and terror, she was completely exhausted.

They burst into the restaurant, shouting; talking over each other; moving at what seemed like impossible speeds. They turned up the lights, exposing the bloodbath before her. Tera was suddenly alerted to some bullet holes in the grand piano's open lid; splintered wood and broken dishes on the floor; blood on the tablecloths; a sea of dead bodies. There was movement from behind the bar, and crying in the kitchen. She had not survived this alone.

Things moved quickly. Tera couldn't remember exactly how she got from the piano bench to the metal chair in the police station, but she could vaguely recall a few things: the helmeted men in blue and black yelling at her; the wailing kitchen staff; some medic who had tried to ask her questions while calming down an injured policeman who was holding his leg and screaming the names of various saints.

Then there were the sirens - bitter oscillating tones, looping out of sync with each other. The intervals and rhythmic patterns flew through Tera's mind like notes on a grand staff; like an incessant etude of dread, involuntarily analyzed by this musician's inner ear, and now infiltrating her mind like some kind of tonal brainwash. This musical torment hypnotically ebbed and flowed as they sped through the city. At least they weren't as loud, she thought, from the inside of the vehicles.

Tera was sitting in a smallish room with dusty grey soundproofing panels on the walls. They looked like they were poorly installed, hastily added over the older construction. Her hands were cuffed, gathered behind the back of her chair. Muffled sounds of hurried activity could just barely be heard through the door behind her. She was being careful to keep her legs from revealing too much skin above the knee, as some of the split skirt of her black dress draped down to the dirty tile floor. Her long black hair was beginning to fall out of its design.

There was a desk between her chair and the three guns who were before her. Two were sitting in their chairs, one was pacing. The light in that room was uncomfortably bright, and she was sure that no amount of makeup could have prepared her for this. She tried to sit up in such a way that would force herself to stay awake. It was a losing battle. She found herself blinking a lot.

The gun on the right was the Sergeant Chief something-or-other-a-relli. Tera didn't quite catch his name.

His face was a tad pudgy with age, probably in his mid-fifties. He was wearing a black police vest. His hair was grey, and he looked serious. He was flipping through papers on a clipboard, double-checking them against a notepad on the desk. He adjusted his reading glasses and cleared his throat. He wrote something down on the first of many forms with his blue ballpoint pen.

The gun on the left was younger. He wore a bulletproof vest over his blue shirt, with a black police cap that covered most of his short light hair. He was leaning forward in his chair and chewing on his pen, eyes bouncing between Tera and the man moving behind him.

The gun pacing the room was tall and thin, dark and mysterious, if not rather imposing. In his late twenties, early thirties. His outfit was notably different from the others, with more of a military look. Tera had to make a conscious effort not to stare at him. She knew that he was the *Tenente*, named Napolitano, because everyone they had walked past to get here had greeted him as such. His pen was behind his right ear.

"What is your name?" asked the right gun.

"Tera Laurito," she said, confidently. Maybe this wouldn't be so hard.

"Do you live in Foggia?"

"Yes,"

"How long have you worked at The Golden Flower?"

"More than a year."

"What is your job?"

"I play the pianoforte," she said, perhaps a little too cheerfully.

"Anything else?"

"I sing sometimes." Maybe she should plead the 5th while she was ahead. She wondered if that would work in Italy. Did they read her any rights?

"What time tonight did you arrive at the restaurant?"

"Around eight... or nine in the evening"

"Can you remember which it was?"

"What?" Tera looked at the guns.

"Can you remember if it was closer to twenty or twenty-one?"

"Ehh…" Tera stared blankly, straight ahead. Unfortunately, straight ahead was the belt of the pacing Lieutenant, who was now standing with his arms crossed between the others. It was a long while before she realized she was staring at his crotch, at which point she quickly closed her eyes, and scrunched up her face a bit. She hoped the awkward situation would fade away, but instead ended up fading herself. The gun on the right snapped his fingers a few times and brought her back to the waking world and the uncomfortably bright lights.

"Urca…" she started suddenly, *"I'm here…"*

"Yes, you are. It is important for you to remember these details."

"Good," she muttered and looked at the gun on the left, who then sat up in his chair. *"What was the question?"* She laughed awkwardly. The three men looked at each other.

*"Is she sober?"*the Lieutenant asked loudly, smacking the left gun on the shoulder, who jumped in his seat.

"Sì..." he responded, looking up at the man.

"Hmm." The Lieutenant looked at Tera and wagged his finger.

"Are you stable?"

*"My mother... yes. Unfortunately,"*she said, suppressing slap-happy giggles within her.

*"What is wrong with you?"*The man was concerned, but mostly annoyed.

*"I haven't slept... in two days,"*she replied.

*"Why haven't you been sleeping?"*asked the older, right gun, in a less harsh manner.

*"I'm a musician."*She said this apologetically, as if it explained everything. "Is it ok if I continue in English? It would be a lot easier for me. *C'è qualcuno che parla inglese?"*

The right gun sighed and shook his head at the others, taking off his glasses. The Lieutenant pursed his lips and replied loudly with a thick accent.

"You are American?"

"Yeah…" she replied.

"Why did you make the choice to live in Italy?"

"It's nice here. I like the food."

"You live in Italy for the food? For the tomatoes?"

"Yeah, I mean, not specifically for the tomatoes, but yeah."

"You have husband here?"

"No..." She was notably less excited now.

"You have parents here?"

"No. They are no longer living."

"You have any family here?"

"I don't think so, but maybe? My..." she paused, "great? Grandfather?" She tapped her high heels on the floor. "I think he was Italian? So..."

"Do you have a violent history?" The man put his hands down on the desk suddenly, forcing the other two men to lean out of the way. The Sgt. Chief on the right looked bothered, while the Sergeant on the left's eyes doubled in size.

"What?" She was still thinking about the tomatoes.

"We found you in the middle of the room surrounded by dead men and women. Did you kill them?" His tone was so dramatic and suddenly angry that Tera started laughing, a bit uncontrollably.

"No!" She knew this wasn't funny, but it just seemed so ridiculous. The three men watched her laugh.

"Signorina Laurito," The left gun joined the conversation. His voice was calm and sympathetic, and his accent wasn't as thick as the Lieutenant's. "Could you please tell us what happened, briefly, and then," he looked at the man looming over him, *"lascia che la signorina riposi?"*

The man in the middle took his hands from the desk and tossed his right hand into the air. He looked at the Sergeant, *"lascia che riposi?"* He sounded disgusted. *"Tu le credi?"* He continued to criticize the light-haired policeman until the Sgt. Chief had to snap his fingers again at Tera to keep her awake. *Tenente* Napolitano looked at Tera, squinted his eyes, then skeptically looked at the Sergeant. He made a sound like, "aight!" and waving his hands, backed up from the desk. He resumed pacing the room, keeping his arms behind his back and his eyes on Tera. She gave him a sheepish smile, blushing a little.

"When you're ready, *Signorina*," the light-haired Sergeant nodded at her. Tera knew she could easily get in trouble for saying the wrong thing. She didn't want to go to Italian prison. However, she did want to help them catch the man who got away. She tried to focus.

"Ok, ok." She started, "I got to work, and things were... normal. I started playing my set, and sometime after... midnight, some of those men from out of town showed up, which was... not normal. Made some of us nervous...I ended my next set and got a drink." She looked at all three of them and slowly explained why she enjoys a white russian on Mondays, especially compared to other mixed drinks, until she realized from the looks on their faces that this detail didn't matter. She continued, "I was sitting in the booth by the window and then they started shooting..."

"Who fired the first shot?" asked the Lieutenant. This interruption really threw off her train of thought.

"I… I have no idea." She rested her head on the back of the chair and looked up at the decorative ceiling tiles. "But…" she smiled, "I know who fired the last ones."

2

Tuesday morning.

They let her sleep for six hours before getting her up again. She woke up under a blanket on a couch in an office, her shoulder being nudged.

"*Buongiorno Signorina, godirebbe una colazione?*"

It was the left gun, kneeling beside her. Behind him, she read backward on the door's glass "*Sovrintendente.*" Two other policemen stood silently in the doorway. Tera's hands were no longer cuffed. She sat up slowly, making sure her dress was decent under the blanket. She carefully moved her hand over her dress. The money was still there, tucked in her bra. Her mind quickly started coming to terms with what was going on. She was still at Police Headquarters. She had witnessed several murders while at work. An Italian cop with light brown hair was offering her a donut.

"*Grazie,*" she took the donut. "Do you have coffee?"

The Sergeant laughed a bit, "*Sempre.*" He waved his hand and held up two fingers to one of the men in the doorway, who nodded and darted off.

"How are you feeling?" he inquired.

"Better than dead," she said, blinking a little. She took a few nibbles of the *ciambella* before the other cop returned with two tiny cups full of strong espresso. The Sergeant handed one to Tera and took the other for himself.

"We need to ask you more questions. Please come with me." He made his way to the door. Tera got up carefully, and followed, munching on the sweet pastry. He walked ahead of her, and the two cops followed behind. So far this experience was surpassing her expectations.

They walked for a bit down the halls in the station before stopping at a door. Inside, it was the same room as last night, but the people were different today. A large man opened the door for them, and a small woman in a suit sat at the desk with a computer. Another, older woman, from the U.S. Consulate stood inside the door and shook Tera's hand as she entered, introducing herself as Mrs. Flora Amenta.

"Accomodati." The light-haired cop motioned to a set of chairs. Tera and Flora sat. He took his seat across from them, next to the petite woman. The large man joined them at the desk and pulled out a chair for himself.

"Miss Laurito," the large man began, in mostly clear English, "I am the *Capo Maresciallo*, Federico Russo. I work for the Italian government." He motioned to his right, *"Sovrintendente,* Luca Conti, *Polizia Centrale di Foggia."* The light-haired cop gave a quick smile. "The *Capo Ispettore*, and my assistant today, Greta Greco." The tiny detective at the computer gave a nod. "And you've already met your Consul." Russo looked nervously at the older woman before turning to some paperwork. Mrs. Amenta said nothing, but looked at the three members of law enforcement with eyes like a hawk. Tera liked her.

He quickly read off a statement filled with boring legal jargon about how Tera had the right to a lawyer, a translator, silence, and other things. She didn't understand all of it, but got the main gist that she didn't have to tell them anything unless she wanted to. The man carried on.

"Right now you are a key witness in the events that took place last night at *Ristorante Fiore Dorato*, between the hours of twenty-three and two. You claim to have spoken to the man who killed Rudolfo Garbazzi, the crime lord more commonly known as 'Garbanzo.' This confrontation led to the death of fourteen others. Your account was verified by three witnesses this morning, that a man entered the restaurant, shots were fired, and the man exited the crime scene alone. While we no longer consider you a primary murder suspect, you are still under our deep consideration. It is critical that you tell us everything you can about who this shooter was. Every detail is important."

"Sure thing," Tera said beneath a yawn, still eating the *ciambella*. "Where should I start?"

"This is very serious, *Signorina*. Are you aware of what I am asking you to do?"

The man was grave. Tera was not. She looked at the three people across from her. The woman was typing, keeping a close eye on Russo. Sergeant Conti was shifting his view between Tera, Flora, and his tiny cup of espresso.

"I've been informed that you have not recently slept well. Are you currently able to understand what is being asked of you?"

Tera leaned back in her chair. She looked blankly at Russo.

"Yes sir," she answered cautiously. Russo nodded. He picked up a folder from the table and waved it slightly.

"This is not the first time you have seen tragedy. You understand the importance of finding justice for those who have lost their loved ones."

"Yes sir," she said coldly.

"Good."

"What would you like to know?" Tera's eyes rested on the folder.

"Let's start with the shooter's appearance. Please, describe how this man looked."

Tera moved her head back and forth a little, still looking at the folder. She let out a sigh.

"He was a bit taller than me… I'd say about... *un metro e ottanta.* He was clean-shaven, had light blonde hair, not too short, but not shaggy. He was built, but not heavy. He looked… quite strong. Didn't seem emotionally connected to anything. He was calm, decisive... very fast." Tera remembered how the man fought the others. There was no competition. "He clearly had combat training…"

She popped the last bit of donut into her mouth as Mrs. Amenta handed her a water bottle. Tera nodded quickly at the older woman before looking back up at Russo. The Chief Marshall clicked his pen in and out a few times.

"Nationality?"

"I'm not sure…"

"Did he look Italian?"

Tera pursed her lips and squinted her eyes, "No, definitely not."

"What color was his skin?"

"He was white. Lighter skin, like me."

"Could you describe his nose?"

"It was… round-ish," she said.

"Eye color?"

"I have no idea - what anyone's eye color is." Tera took a sip of water. The tiny woman continued to type. Sergeant Conti leaned back in his chair.

"Could you give a guess?" Russo asked.

"I really don't know," she said.

"Did you get a look at his teeth?"

"What?" she asked.

"His teeth. Did you get a look at his teeth?"

"Oh, um, no."

"What was he wearing?"

Tera tried to concentrate, placing herself back into the restaurant.

"Dark pants, a lighter colored dress shirt, maybe… short-sleeved. No coat. Most of his arms were exposed. And he had dark gloves."

"Footwear?"

"Black shoes... maybe boots."

"Did he have any visible tattoos, jewelry, or other notable characteristics?"

She couldn't recall anything specific to answer this question. She tried to remember if the man had a watch on his wrist when he held up his gun. She could still remember his mannerisms, and wondered if there was a way to communicate those to the police, in any tangible way. She could easily picture how he blinked, how he moved his head. The way he moved his lips when he spoke. He had a way of staring you down that reminded her of an instructor she once had in music school. Based on the way he moved, she suspected he had good balance. She also intrinsically felt that he might be a dancer. There were a hundred little things like this that she didn't know how to tell the Chief Marshall.

"No," she said.

"How old was he?"

"He was old-ish..." her face scrunched up with indecision.

"What does that mean?" asked Russo.

"Well, he was certainly older than me. So, I don't know, somewhere between thirty and fifty-five."

"That's quite a range. Can you narrow it down?"

Tera looked at the Chief Marshall.

"Oh, I don't know... How old are you?" she asked.

"Forty-seven," he said, blankly.

"Ok, well, he looked about your age."

"Alright. What language did he speak?"

"*Italiano*... uh, and English," she recalled.

"Did he have a discernible accent?"

Tera started counting on her fingers.

"Well, he said like, nine words to me, so it's hard to say. I would guess that he was not a native Italian speaker. His English sounded... formal. He was probably British, or maybe American?"

"Why do you think he might have been American?" Russo sounded intrigued - his eyes bouncing between Tera and Ms. Amenta.

"I don't know. I guess because of the song he wanted me to play. It's an American song, but that doesn't mean that he was an American."

"What song?"

"Iris," Tera smirked. "He wanted me to play Iris."

"What exactly did he say to you?"

"He asked me if I worked for Garbazzi...I told him I was the piano player. He asked to make a song request. And he had a gun. So I didn't say no. Then he looked at me and just said, 'Iris,' so I started to play."

Russo nodded and began to look through some papers on the table before turning to the tiny woman next to him.

"*Dove sono le mappe?*" he asked through a sigh. The woman opened her own briefcase and took out a series of diagrams.

"*In bianco?*" she asked him.

"*Sì.*" He waved his hand at her, reaching for the paper. He looked it over briefly before placing the crude paper map of the restaurant onto the desk in front of Tera. It showed the kitchen, the exits, the bar, the piano, and had little red "x" marks where each dead body was found.

"How did he enter the room?" he asked.

"I don't know... by the time I was aware of him, he had just shot the two men behind... the bar," she pointed to the paper map, "so he was near the piano. He was coming from the direction of the front door, I believe. And, he was there," she tapped the paper "in the middle of the room by the bar, when I lost sight of him.

"Did he give any indication of where he was going?"

"What?" Tera looked amused. "No... he left that bit out."

"Did he have anything with him other than his gun?"

"He took a cigarette...off Garbazzi, after he shot him."

"Anything else?"

"I don't think so."

"Did he show any signs of injury?"

"I don't think so."

"Did he take his gun with him?"

"I don't... hmm..." Tera paused. She remembered watching him set the money on the piano. At that time he was still holding a gun. She never saw him drop it. Never heard him set it down.

"Yes, I think he took it with him."

"Do you remember what kind of gun he had?"

"It was a handgun. A Pistol."

"Do you remember any other details about the gun?"

"No," she said. This was a lie, as she immediately remembered several other details about the gun. Details she didn't want to remember, like the sound of the shots being fired, or the click of a new magazine. She remembered the way he held the gun, aimed the gun, lowered the gun. She remembered the smells of the smoking metal, of the alcohol, and the sweat. The memories washed over her in a flash that made her feel sick.

"As a gun owner yourself, *Signorina*, would you be able to identify this man's gun in a photograph?"

"Possibly." She looked up. "The room wasn't well lit."

They spent the next hour and a half trying to help her remember the exact sequence of events - such as the order in which the men arrived, and the order in which the men were shot. Then she told them what she could remember about the people involved, including her boss who was killed in the crossfire. Remembering all of this was heartbreaking, and very difficult for Tera to talk about, so she chose her words sparingly, asking not to be pressed on it.

Eventually they made their way to the topic of her music, and the questioning ended on a lighter note - with a brief conversation about the Goo Goo Dolls, and whether or not their songs were worth listening to.

3

Russo gave Tera a card for a local therapist. He recommended that she meet with someone as soon as possible, and as often as needed. He instructed Tera to remain in Foggia until further notice. She was not to leave Italy for any reason. She was not to talk to strangers. She needed to be careful and stay out of trouble. They would be in touch.

Tera and Flora were escorted out to the lobby where they sat in metal chairs and waited. They were seated across from two State policemen: an old fat cop and a young scraggly cop with a mustache. They sat quietly, processing and exchanging awkward glances. There were other cops in the lobby who stood near the building entrance; younger men, wearing black instead of blue. They stood with their hands behind their backs. They wore tall black boots and had white belts across their chests. Well built. Looked more serious. Tera could read on their jackets that they were *Carabinieri* - the military police.

Flora put her hand on Tera's shoulder and assured her that everything would be alright. She gave her a card in case she needed any help finding an English speaking lawyer. Tera tried to listen politely to Flora, but was distracted by some distant voices; she could just barely make out a conversation from down the hall:

"You let her sleep in your office? Unsupervised?"

"I kept the door locked."

"Have you no sense whatsoever of protocol?" This man's tone was full of anger.

"What were we supposed to do? She was falling asleep between words, she was clearly exhausted. The lady needed to rest."

"You should have gotten creative, found ways to keep her awake!"

"You want me to torment the young woman? Slap her around like I would a man? She was not well. She needed to sleep."

"Then you should have kept her in a cell until morning!"

"A cell? Pig cow... a cell is so uncomfortable. It is for lawbreakers. Why should we have locked her up when the others were allowed to go to the hospital?"

"Shame on you, Conti. It is evident that you are not used to handling situations at this level of priority! What if she is working with the killer? Or what if the killer had come here, to silence the young woman's testimony? Then you should have locked her up for her own safety!"

Tera swallowed nervously and combed through her long dark hair with her hands, looking between the police agents across from her. After some time, Sgt. Conti came out into the lobby. He straightened his police cap with both hands and walked over to the counter. A man behind a glass window handed him a long black coat and a large envelope. He looked at Tera and the U.S. Consulate representative, nodded, and handed Tera the coat and envelope. He took a card out of his pocket and gave it to her saying, "If you need to get a hold of us, call me. I speak English." He smiled.

The mustachioed cop stood up - he and the older police agent escorted Tera out to a blue State Police car. They drove in silence until Tera asked them if she could be dropped off a few blocks away from her apartment, to not draw attention. They agreed and let her out where she asked.

She walked the familiar streets up to her building, weaving in and out of the skinny trees, parked cars, and scooters in the tight streets between the beautifully bright colored apartments and businesses. She looked up at the laundry hanging on the old balconies, and the potted green plants draping from the windows. She ignored the graffiti on the otherwise pretty stone walls. Tera dug her key out of the envelope that her personal effects had been gathered in, and unlocked the big front door to the lobby. It was all so familiar, yet once again foreign. So much had happened since she last came home.

She quietly climbed the old marble staircase up to the third floor, unlocked her door, and stepped inside. She set the envelope, her coat, and her phone onto the piano bench in the small front room and headed left to the bedroom and bath. After a long shower, she plopped down on the twin-sized bed and stared up at the broken ceiling fan. Her phone began to buzz in the other room. After a whimper, she got up from the bed and went to get her phone. It was an alarm, reminding her to go to her hair appointment today.

"*Mannaggia...*" she murmured. She had dinner plans too. And a gig to play tomorrow. And another this weekend. Should she clear her schedule? Everything had only just happened in the last twelve hours. She was still in shock, hardly processing any of it.

But Tera hated limitations. She thought about this while she walked into the hair salon. Elena greeted her.

*"How's it going?"*Elena asked with a big smile.

"Fine." Like hell.

"How is work?"

*"It's good."*Except my boss is dead. Tera looked around the room. *"Slow day?"* They were the only two in the small salon.

*"Patrizia is sick today,"*said the hairdresser, *"and Silvia is in Russia until Monday..."*

Tera took a seat in a salon chair while Elena went on about how Silvia is always traveling. Tera flipped through a fashion catalog until she found what she was looking for. She showed Elena, who nodded with excitement.

*"Yes! Yes, this is very popular."*She went to a nearby shelf full of hair products.

"Hmm.... I know I have more of this color, in the back. One minute."

Elena disappeared behind a swinging door into the back storage area of the salon. Tera sat, spinning in her chair, looking at the empty room. The walls were brick, painted black with hot pink and neon green accents. There were a few large banners that hung near the product shelves, featuring computer-generated faces with random design collages exploding around their heads instead of hair. Large potted plants filled in what spaces were otherwise unoccupied, and three ceiling fans were spinning and humming along with the Italian pop music.

Large storefront windows were pouring natural light into the little salon; every now and then someone on the street outside would walk past. Tera started to read an article about how celebrities deal with hair loss. She heard the door chime, but didn't pay any attention to who had walked in. She looked at the hair catalog, until the man who had entered the salon stood in front of her. She looked up to see an older man in a big brown coat, his hands in his pockets. He smiled, and though he looked very Italian, he spoke in English with an American accent.

"Hello, Tera." He spoke slowly, "My employer asked me to relay a message to you. It's very important." She suddenly felt incredibly uncomfortable. Very alone. Defenseless. She set down the catalog on the counter behind her, carefully sliding the styling shears into her coat sleeve with her other hand. She had done sleight-of-hand like this before with silverware, mostly spoons, as a bar trick. She wasn't sure what good sense inside her prompted this reaction, but she felt proud of herself.

"Last night you saw a man leave the *Fiore Dorato,* and no doubt, the police have probably asked you to return to them, so as to identify that man. When that happens, we simply ask that you forget what he looked like. Do this for us, and we'll be out of your hair..." He lifted his left hand out of his pocket and waved it around the room with another big smile. He was wearing a brown leather glove. "You can forget about us, and we will forget about you." He slowly lifted his right hand out of his pocket, revealing a thick, black, semi-automatic pistol. He casually tapped it against his side.

"Or," he persisted, still smiling, "if you decide to tell the police about me, anything I've said, or if you decide to identify that man," he tilted his head, "then things might become a little difficult for you."

Tera kept a straight face and calm composure, mostly out of denial. She was pretty sure this wasn't actually happening. Perhaps he was a paid actor.

"I have a question," she asked, casually. The man seemed curious. Tera continued to spin back and forth slightly in the chair.

"Why don't you just... kill me? Wouldn't that be easier for you?" She spoke with confidence but soon felt her legs begin to shake slightly, as her nerves were beginning to catch up with the facts: what was happening wasn't imaginary. She stopped spinning - her body was now filling up with all the tension from the room.

"Oh, Tera," the man began to say, in a condescending voice, "don't say that. We're not monsters. We would prefer that nobody have to die. Just do like I asked, and we won't have to worry about you, or your loved ones back in the States."

Tera laughed quietly to herself.

"I'm afraid you're only threatening me here. My loved ones are already dead."

She looked the man in the face, with a confidence that made him feel a little nervous, though he hid it well behind another big fake smile.

"Well, I'm sorry to hear that. But we know you care about your friends."

Tera felt her face lose its color. She wasn't without friends. There were plenty of people in Italy that she would hate to see hurt.

"Oh, one more thing," he started to slowly put the gun back in his pocket. "Don't try to run away," he waved his left hand around again, and spoke like he was telling an exaggerated story, "or stay in a hotel… thinking that we won't know where you are. Just, do as I said, and we'll leave you alone." He gave a slight bow and turned to the door. "Have a nice day, *Signorina* Laurito."

She watched the man leave the store. He straightened his coat collar with both hands and looked back at her through the window before walking away, joining the clueless citizens of the city plaza. Tera was left once again in the empty room, with the humming fans and the music.

She felt like she had just been punched in the stomach, and while she felt little to no distinct emotion at this moment, a few tears began to leak out of both eyes. She pushed back hard, stuffing every thought deep inside, pretending nothing had just happened. She put the scissors back on the counter and picked up the catalog again. Seconds later, Elena emerged from the back room with a box, a little flustered.

"You won't believe this!" She laughed. "I got myself locked in the supply closet! Isn't that wild? I don't know what I would have done if I hadn't had my keys with me."

4

Tera had a slight change of plans at the salon. She ended up going way shorter than she had initially desired, but for some reason it made her quite happy to look dramatically different. Elena had fun adding all of the colors into Tera's dark hair, bringing out highlights, blending in purple and red. The end result looked less crazy than you'd think. It was actually very chic. Tera hugged Elena before leaving.

"*I'm glad you're ok,*" she said, giving her a kiss on both cheeks. Elena was a little confused, but smiled and waved as Tera walked out the door and down the street. Tera had a fresh sense about her. Still stuffing all thoughts about the last twenty-four hours, she focused on her reflection in the storefront windows, checking herself out with her new look.

She was able to walk five blocks before she noticed a man in a dark leather coat, who seemed to be keeping even pace with her. She took a break from walking - sat on a bench in a piazza near a fountain. The fountain was off, which wasn't very charming at all. She watched some birds dance around the locals, who rode through the piazza with baskets and luggage attached to their bikes. It was cloudy today and a little on the chill side. She tried not to look at the man in the leather jacket, which actually became very easy since he had completely disappeared. She scanned the piazza. It might have been her imagination. Either way, it was probably stupid for her to be out alone. She got up from the bench and began walking toward a nearby pastry shop. She didn't know it, but a man in the piazza followed after her.

Tera walked up to the pastry counter and stared at all the wondrous options.

"*Buon pomeriggio,*" the large woman behind the counter greeted her. Tera would have smiled, but her face seemed temporarily incapable of doing this. She stared intently at the pastries. Perhaps one of these sweet items could serve as a magic potion, to heal her mind - allow her to think straight. But she needed to get the right one. Only the right one would be able to take away the pain welling up inside of her. Calm her nerves. Assure her that everything was alright. A skinny kid behind the counter waved at Tera.

"*Ciao maestra!*" He said cheerfully. Tera looked up. She recognized the kid. She had given him piano lessons last summer. She had to think for a few seconds before remembering his name.

"*Loreto, how are you? Have you been practicing?*" Social habit was winning over her psyche. For exactly ten seconds, she forgot about everything else, thinking only of Loreto and the time they had spent together learning etudes. But then his large mother looked at Tera closely, and recognizing her, she gasped.

"*Signorina Laurito…*" she whispered loudly and left a customer at the register in the middle of a transaction.

"*Ehi!*" The lady at the register threw her hands in the air, waving some paper euros.

"*Vuoi i miei soldi?*" she exclaimed, all bothered.

Loreto's mother didn't care and waved the lady away. A short, older man walked in from the piazza as the lady at the register stuffed her euros into the tip jar, took her bag of sweets, and left the shop. The large woman leaned across the counter and whispered at Tera.

"*I heard about The Golden Flower...*" she said. "*Do you know? Riccardo Di Maggio was good friends with my husband. This is so terrible. Have you been told what happened?*"

Tera looked at the woman, and at her skinny son.

"No," she looked down at the floor, solemn.

"*So terrible,*" the woman was shaking her head. "*Riccardo was a good man.*"

"*Sì,*" Tera nodded at the floor, still unsure whether or not her boss was actually dead, or if this was just an elaborate ruse.

"*To think,*" the woman lamented, "*that this could happen to us here in Foggia. It's so terrible.*"

"*Sì...*" Tera said.

"*And poor Carlos, he is so young I think, to now manage the business.*"

The short man took a seat in an empty booth by the door, keeping his eyes on Tera, but occasionally looking out the store's windows to the street.

"*Do you know how long it will be before they will reopen the restaurant?*" the woman asked, still speaking in hushed tones.

"*I do not,*" Tera said. "*So, if you know anyone who is hiring,*" she shrugged at the two of them behind the counter, who were nodding.

"*We could put a piano in here!*" Loreto said, with a small laugh. His mother smiled at him.

"*Yes, yes. You would be an excellent pianist for our shop, Loreto! Anything you want.*" She patted her son on the back, knocking him back and forth with the force of her love. He laughed some more, nervously. They packed up a few treats and gave them to Tera at no charge. She thanked them and walked towards the door. The short man stood up,

"*Signorina,*" he tipped his hat to her.

"*I couldn't help but hear that you are looking for work?*" he got a little closer, "*I wanted to tell you,*" he said in a lowered voice, "*there is a man outside who is following you. I am a police agent. May I walk you home?*" He proudly showed her an old badge in his coat, which read "*Polizia di Stato, Reparto a Cavallo.*"

Tera was immediately charmed by the image of this little man on a horse. She nodded and thanked him. They walked out together, joining a group of older women.

"*Mia moglie,*" he introduced his wife, "*le sue sorelle,*" her sisters, "*e il nostro amico*" and their friend. Together they walked around the piazza. They visited a few vendors before eventually walking the ten blocks back to Tera's apartment. She thanked them all and waved goodbye from inside the locked lobby door. She journeyed up the stairs to her apartment and shut herself in.

She peered out her windows to the streets below. Beneath the neighboring balconies and various trees she was able to make out a decent amount of foot traffic. But she didn't see the man in the leather jacket. She saw ten men in leather jackets. And they all looked suspicious… getting into their cars. Waiting for the bus. Riding their bikes.

She addressed her paranoia head-on and quickly affixed all three of the clunky safety locks on her door. She wasn't sure why there were so many added locks slapped onto the wall, but it made her feel a little bit safer to have them all latched in that rickety old building. She buried herself in her couch; Tera was done for the day.

Her arm slowly stretched out from beneath the pillow she was clutching and clamored clumsily for her phone. She needed to text Maria and cancel their dinner plans.

Maria was easily Tera's best friend in Italy. After moving to Foggia, Tera unearthed one of those rare Italian evangelical Christian communities, and quickly felt at home within the walls of the tiny, garage-like church. This was where she met Maria.

Tera and Maria were both begrudgingly a part of the cluster of single women who sat together every Sunday morning - strategically, to help ward off the single men in the congregation. The single men at that church were charming fellows, but they were mostly in their sixties, divorced, and former drug addicts saved through the local mission. Tera tried to stay clear of them, though their testimonies were actually quite inspirational.

Then there was Matteo, the pastor's son. Matteo was not old or anything, but he was a bit odd. He had a handsome face, albeit a little crooked when he smiled - which was often - but he wasn't much of a leader and was often annoying - Tera thought. Perhaps this was because he was very much in love with both Tera and Maria.

Every Sunday Matteo would invite one or both of them to his family's house for Sunday dinner. Whenever they would decline, he would bother Maria's younger sisters - she had three of them - and tell them about how great he was. He would also talk about why they should all go fishing with him. Neither Tera or Maria liked fish, fishing, or water. Matteo knew this. Yet he confidently persisted.

Tera and Maria found great solace in each other, often commiserating on the many things that bothered them. Maria spoke English, and like Tera, had strong convictions. But apart from the few things they had in common, they were clear opposites. Tera was quiet; Maria was loud. Tera didn't like to plan things, while Maria literally ran her own home business - selling handmade napkins around the world. When Tera was down, Maria knew how to cheer her up. When Maria was bored, Tera made her life more interesting. Tera was often asking Maria for advice on money, marketing, makeup, and men.

Tera started the text:

I need to cancel our dinner. My life is in danger and I'm afraid to leave my apartment.

She looked at her phone. She hit the back button, erasing the second sentence. She started to type again.

A strange man is following me.

She looked at her phone for another second before deleting that as well. After a thought, she left her finger on the key long enough to delete the entire message. She heard footsteps outside her door. There was a timid knock.

"*Signorina Laurito?*" It was the voice of *Signor* Lombardo.

"*I don't want to be involved, but I heard about the massacre...*" Tera quietly undid all the locks and opened the door a bit. "*Mrs. Bianchi told me,*" he said, quietly, as Tera peered at her nosy neighbor through the skinny crack of the open door. The peculiar man had a tablet in his hand, with a news article about the shooting. "*I looked it up.*" He showed her the tablet. Her eyes widened at the sight of the headline, and she quickly looked away. "*I don't want to be involved, but I wanted to know if you were ok.*"

Tera knew that Sig. Lombardo used to be a reporter before he retired. She was sure he would want to write about this for his blog.

"*Thank you for your concern,*" she said, "*But I do not want to talk about it now.*" She closed the door as he was raising his right hand with more questions.

"*Signorina, permettimi!*" he continued through the door. Tera heard the sound of the downstairs neighbor calling up to him,

"*What is going on up there?*"

It was only a matter of time before there were three or four other neighbors standing outside Tera's door, reading Sig. Lombardo's tablet, knocking and calling to Tera through her flimsy thin door. Maybe going out for dinner wasn't such a bad idea after all. Tera texted Maria that she "might have some company" with her tonight, figuring that "company" would cover any unexpected men with guns, tag-a-long neighbors, or other unexpected visitors. She thought about the kind-hearted horse-cop who walked her home. Maybe getting an escort was a good idea. So she hesitantly called Matteo.

5

The sounds of the anxious Italians continued to fill the stairwell, coming through the thin, thin walls. Tera decided that now was a good time to check through her apartment for invaders, bugs, bombs, and weak spots. The conversations outside her door weren't offering her any comfort... her neighbors wondering whether or not their town was being overrun with gangs, clans, or crime syndicates...

Tera was quickly losing any sense of home or peace for this apartment. She didn't even feel safe in her own bed. Every square inch was trying to kill her. After checking for bugs behind every book on her shelf, she opened her piano bench, only to immediately start judging which music inside was worth keeping. Yes, moving was probably in her best interest now.

It had hardly been the fifteen minutes that Matteo had estimated - before he was calling through the door with the others. Tera didn't really want him around, but figured it was safer than being alone. And it made more sense to have him following her than a mob of questioning elders. She opened the door and let him slide in, trying her best to shoo the others away.

"*Mia cara! Sei la mia vita...*" he put his hands on Tera's arms for a moment, affectionately, if not trepidatiously. Italians are physical people, and Tera typically was not. Matteo knew this, and in case he forgot, Tera was currently emitting an aura that said: "touch me and die." Their interactions were often a strange combination of differing cultures, the one-sided romantic interest, and his overly emotional personality. Matteo proceeded to wave his hands in all directions, spouting words of worry and relief, interjected with platitudes and mild expletives. In a normal relationship, or even a more normal friendship, there would have been a hug at some point. But after a minute, Matteo was left looming awkwardly nearby. And as if just now looking at her, he quietly reached out and touched her hair.

"This is so different..." He had a look of wonder and concern on his face.

"It is something I always wanted to do," she said, defensively, batting him away. She motioned to the piano bench, then quickly pushed the mess of loose sheet music off of the sofa, and sat down. Matteo sat on the bench for exactly one second before springing up again and pacing about the room with his hands in motion.

"*Ma, cosa ha detto la polizia? Come è potuto accadere? Nella nostra piccola città...*" He went on and on, with no signs of stopping. This wasn't a surprise, but it was very annoying.

"Oh honestly..." Tera said quietly. He stood near the door, letting his hands drop to his side, before quickly folding his arms across his chest.

"You sound like *Signora* Bianchi." She pointed to the ceiling emphatically, before letting her hand drop into the remaining papers next to her. Since Matteo arrived, a few of the neighbors had had the good sense to leave them alone. There were only a few hushed voices in the stairwell now.

"What I need from you right now is... is..." she waved her hands in front of her in a circular motion, "Help me calm my mind." She rested her hands on her lap, palms up. Matteo nodded, working hard to follow her English. "I'm very nervous. And I am afraid. And I hate being afraid, Matteo." She stared intently at her piano. There was more anger behind her look than fear. Silence fell on the apartment... with only some muffled chatter slowly fading away through the door. Sig.ra. Bianchi could be heard loudly whispering to Sig.ra. Gabrielli before a few doors closed shut.

"What can I do for you?" Matteo said, slower, almost like a sigh.

"Well..." she looked about the room, trying to decide where to start.

"I would like to keep quiet about the shooting, as much as possible," realizing as she said it that she was facing incredible opposition to this goal.

"You would like to keep...?" Matteo's English wasn't very good, but he was trying.

"Um..." she continued anyway, *"If you could please... stay close to me during dinner, and..."* She immediately caught herself, as he let out a hopeful smile,

"Not too close!" she added, pointing her finger at him firmly. *"only stay close enough, so that I am not alone in a dark alleyway,"* She scratched her head, "or, in any overt danger, you know?"

Matteo nodded, and looked from side to side before asking, "What is, 'o-vert' meaning?"

"Um… *evidente… non in pericolo evidente.*"

"*Sì, sì.*" He nodded and looked worried. "You are… in overt danger?"

"Well, I hope not… I mean, no. No." She stared deep into the rug, which now lay crooked across the floor. She thought of the man in the salon with the gun, and how someone had been following her only hours ago. How she was probably being watched right now. She tried to keep flashes of memory from last night out of her head, but even the sounds of footsteps reminded her of gunfire. It took all her concentration to focus on what sounds were actually in the room… to blot out the sounds in her memory by honing in only on what was occurring now, in reality in front of her.

"Maybe it is best if we do not go out tonight?" Matteo said, *"We can ask Maria to meet us here. I will call her."*

"No," she shook her head, *"I need to be able to leave without being afraid. And I am very afraid of staying here and being safe."*

"I do not understand." A phrase Matteo confidently knew how to say in English. Tera closed her eyes for a moment, then stared straight at Matteo, with boldness.

"Sometimes being afraid to live your life is worse than being shot." She said this so coldly that Matteo gulped, and looked both intimidated and impressed. Tera stood up and went to the door.

They left the apartment and proceeded down the old staircase into the dirty, ornate lobby and out the large wooden doors to the street. The sun had just started to disappear behind the horizon, and the temperature was beginning to cool off to what could now be described as chilly. Matteo offered his arm, but Tera shook her head.

6

Tera and Matteo walked four blocks to a little restaurant, where Maria was waiting for them. Maria, though quite clever, didn't often follow the news and somehow had not yet heard about the shooting.

Her eyes lit up when she saw Tera's hair, and she spent the first several minutes talking about it. She seemed disappointed to see Matteo. She had been hoping for someone more interesting to be "the company" coming along for the evening. Like maybe a couple of handsome musicians. But she slowly warmed up to him being there.

They sat in a corner, by a stone fireplace, ordered a round of drinks. It was cozy, and felt safe enough. The windows on the opposite wall overlooked the street, where some small groups of people slowly made their way through the town - silhouettes in the streetlight. There were fewer cars on the roads now, with mostly bikes and scooters whizzing about.

"So..." Maria began, in her heavy Italian accent. "What is new?" She held onto the stem of her wine glass and leaned back in her chair, skeptically eyeing Tera and Matteo who both looked concerned. Matteo turned to Tera, unsure what to say.

"I need a new job," Tera said blankly.

Maria lowered her glass and raised her eyebrows.

"And I think I'll be moving soon," Tera continued, "perhaps to somewhere on the west coast."

"But you just got here!" Maria sat up, putting down the drink. "No, don't move away! All my friends move away. If you move away," Maria reached out her hand and set it in the middle of the table, "then I am going to go with you. I am tired of everyone else moving away."

"Ok," Tera smiled slightly. "That's fine with me. We can be roommates in *Napoli*."

"Yes!" Maria said. "And you can play the piano for me while I complain about my job!" She smiled big across the table. Then, looking at Matteo,

"And how about you? Are you going to move with us too? Leave your mother and father behind?"

"*Mah...*" Matteo shrugged and put his hands in the air. *"Non lo so."* He looked at Tera and then at Maria. *"You really want to move?"* He scratched his head. *"I guess if you go to the west coast, I could visit. Visiting is much easier than leaving Foggia."* He looked at Tera. *"Why don't you stay? We can help you find a new job."*

Tera and Maria looked at Matteo.

"You do not even have a job, how can you help?" Maria said, almost smacking over a water glass. Matteo ignored her.

"You haven't lived here very long..." he said.

Tera looked at both of them, a little annoyed.

"I'm just... trying to be realistic. There aren't very many jobs left for a pianist in this town. *Fiore Dorato* was a steady gig, and most of my income."

"What happened with *Fiore Dorato?* Did you have to quit?" Maria asked.

Tera and Matteo exchanged looks. "I don't want to talk about it yet…" Tera said, seriously.

"Hmm… well, you could teach again?" Maria bounced in her seat. "I know many people who would love to learn the piano."

"Yes, but how many people in Foggia are willing to pay my fee for lessons?" Tera asked. "I've been down that road before. This just isn't a good location for teaching lessons at a living wage. I need to go somewhere with a richer population."

"Yes, yes. You say this a lot…" Maria pondered. The waiter returned to the table, but it was clear that no one was ready to order. But he didn't mind. He would help them decide, now, what to eat. Partway through his insistence for the soup, Matteo stopped him.

"*Deve ancora arrivare un altra persona.*" He said, with his hand up.

"What?" asked Maria. "*Chi?*"

"*Cosa?*" Matteo looked playful. "*Il tuo ragazzo sta ancora arrivando, giusto?*"

"My what? You invited someone for me?" Maria looked angry. She gasped,

"*I do not want Lorenzo! You tell him to leave me alone!*" She stood up. She started wagging her finger at Matteo. "*You call him right now! You tell him to go home to his sisters, I am not interested!*"

The waiter backed off as Matteo stood up too.

"What's your problem? Why are you yelling at me?" Matteo whined.

Things typically escalated quickly with these two. Lorenzo was one of Matteo's Catholic fishing buddies. Maria didn't like Catholics. This was a big part of why she was still single.

Tera rested her head in her hand with her arm on the table and stared blankly through the three of them, out the far windows to the street. As Matteo and Maria began to slap each other's hands in a gesticulation battle, Tera began scanning for threats. Were there men out there watching them? Was the man with the leather jacket hiding behind some tourist guidebook, or standing against some building? Lighting a cigarette? Drawing a gun? Was she putting her friends in needless danger by being with them in public? The obnoxious feeling of "being in danger" that she had spent years learning to shed in America was once again taking a hold of her life. Her best response to overcoming this crippling fear was, and still is, with anger. Anger is stronger than fear.

"I'll have the soup!" Tera was loud and stern. Stern enough to stop her friends' argument cold; Tera was rarely loud, and this legitimately surprised them. The waiter gave a slight bow, then scurried off to the kitchen, disregarding the others. Maria sat down slowly.

"Something is not right," she said to Tera. Matteo scratched his head, looking at the two of them, waiting it seemed, for someone to tell him what to do.

"*Is someone else coming?*" Tera asked Matteo.

"No..." he looked at Maria, "*Scusa.*"

He took his seat.

"What is going on?" Maria asked, a little frustrated. "What happened with your job?"

"I really don't want to talk about it." Tera's hands hovered over the table, then, after a grunt, she pulled up the article on her phone about the shooting and pushed it across to Maria. Maria looked at the phone, a little confused at first, then her eyes opened wide, and she looked at Tera with astonishment. Tera leaned forward and rested her head in both hands.

"It happened so quick, you know. I spent all night, well, all morning, really... down there at the police station..." she pointed to the wall. They both nodded at her. "...trying to answer all of these questions about what happened... in what order... with all the details... It was really tiring and difficult." Tera slid her spoon in and out of her coat sleeve, "But yeah, fifteen people... Right there. In front of... me."

"*Oddio...*" Maria muttered.

"*I know, right?*" Matteo said to Maria. "*Some gang shows up in our town, and what was it... Were there six locals who were killed?*"

"They were caught in the wrong place at the wrong time." Tera looked distant.

"*But how lucky is it, that Tera is ok?*"

"It wasn't luck, it was the hand of God..." Maria spoke quietly.

"That's what I meant..." Matteo said, a little embarrassed. *"But you were not hurt, were you?"*

"Yeah… I'm fine. A number of people survived without injury. But some police got hurt pretty bad. Carlos is ok… he hid behind the bar, ran into the kitchen. Well, I should say that he wasn't physically hurt… his father was killed..."

"Carlos is…?" Maria started to ask.

"Carlos Di Maggio," Matteo jumped in. *"Riccardo Di Maggio era suo padre. Suo padre era il proprietario del Fiore Dorato"*

Matteo was doing his best to sound informed, but he didn't know much about what happened, and the news articles didn't have much in the way of details yet.

"He's nineteen years old," Tera added.

"Wow…" Maria shook her head. "Just, just, wow." She looked at the article with her hand on her mouth. *"I knew them..."* she gasped, tapping the phone. *"I knew Thomas and Stefano, from the book store... they were both killed. This is terrible..."*

They sat for a few minutes in silence as Maria read through the article, again and again.

"When did you get home? Did you get any rest?" Matteo asked Tera.

"I slept for a few hours at the police station. Got home around eleven this morning."

The three of them sat quietly until the waiter brought Tera some soup. Tera stared at it for a long time before finally eating it. Matteo ordered some pasta dish, but Maria said she wasn't hungry. Matteo made her order dessert.

"How are you dealing with this?" Maria looked at Tera, still totally in shock. Tera looked back with a dull expression.

"Honestly, I'm trying not to think about it."

"Will you have to testify at court?" she asked.

"Maybe... I don't know. They told me not to leave the city."

"*Oddio...*" Maria shook her head and looked over at Matteo. He looked awkwardly at both of them until they finished eating.

Matteo's father's credit card picked up the check. They all walked Tera home, passing through various clouds of cigarette smoke from the few groups of youth who were jammed around the disco entrances that lined the alleys.

Tera didn't make any mention of the shooter, the man at the salon, or anything that happened that afternoon. She felt distant, keeping so many secrets from her friends. Even so, it helped to talk about what she could. She knew that her official therapy sessions would start tomorrow morning and she knew a bit of what to expect. She'd gone through those before. The government tries to help people like Tera sort out their tragic lives in a safe and confidential environment.

Looking up at her friends while they walked her home, Tera realized that even in a "safe" place, she wouldn't be able to talk about the man at the salon without pulling them into harm's way. She would have to keep that a secret for much longer. Possibly her whole life.

7

Wednesday.

Tera spent that night awake in her bed, thinking about Monday night. She thought about the shooter. She thought about the questions she was asked by the police, and the answers she gave. Had she forgotten anything? She thought about all the people at the restaurant. She thought about the attractive Lieutenant who was yelling at her about the tomatoes. She remembered what it was like to first move to Italy, to find work, and move to Foggia. She remembered meeting Maria and instantly becoming best friends while eating dinner with her family after church. Somehow these thoughts took up the entire night, because the sun was rising before she knew it.

What had only been local news yesterday had quickly become national, and the story of the Foggia massacre, or *"Strage di Foggia,"* became international overnight. Now every television in Italy was showing footage of the *Fiore Dorato,* alongside interviews with politicians, statements from police commissioners, and a public address from the Pope. Foggia had entered the media spotlight.

They were calling it "inter-criminal conflict over drug trades," with fifteen dead and six injured. It was the biggest massacre in Italy since 1998, when some idiot

American pilots from the Marine Corp accidentally took out an aerial cable car in Cavalese, killing twenty. The last big shooting in Italy was in 2008 when the Casalesi clan killed six African immigrants and one Italian. From what Tera could tell, few details had been released about the *Strage di Foggia*, apart from the death toll and the unnerving headlines of *"Killer at Large," "Manhunt underway,"* and *"Mysterious International Gunman Missing."*

Something that no one on the news was talking about was the psychological damage. One of the hardest parts of overcoming tragedy is figuring out how to do the simple things, like how to get out of bed. It's tricky, because you need to have a reason to get out of bed. Fear and sorrow have a way of removing all reason. Tera thought about getting up, for about an hour, before moving an inch. She had to force herself to sit up. She found that she was already becoming frustrated with herself for missing the upcoming counseling appointment, two hours from now. But Tera encouraged this kind of self-hate within herself. She knew from experience that she could use it as a motivating force. So she refused to let herself be late and used this determination to get out of bed.

She got dressed, ate a quick breakfast, and grabbed her phone and coat. If she could get herself moving, she could overcome the desire to stay inside all day. She could overcome that pull to go back to bed. She could use these habits to keep herself from reliving the pain of her past. She hated the idea of being so helpless.

Despite her best efforts, she wound up being late to her appointment anyway, as she walked clear past the building where the meeting was, and ended up circling around several blocks trying to find it. She eventually swallowed her pride and called the number on the business card. A social worker, named Tiziano, found her outside and ushered her into the clinic. He was a skinny older man with big eyes under big round glasses, spazzy grey hair, and dark skin. His smile took up his entire face. He introduced Tera to *Dottoressa* Fabrizia Giuliani, who would now be her "coach." She was a kind woman with big hair, a big nose, and very white teeth. Her English was not bad. It was sometimes a little confusing, but it was not bad. She told Tera "It's ok. We have some English." Tera smiled and said, "I'm sure you do."

They sat in her cozy office, exchanging casual conversation in both languages, getting to know each other a little. They spent an hour talking about Tera. They talked about her interests, her church, her favorite foods. They did not talk about her past. They did not talk about the shooting. Tera wondered if this was a strategic approach to trauma therapy, or if this was an oversight. Then Fabrizia got up and opened the door.

"That's it, then?" Tera asked.

"Oh, no," Dott.ssa Giuliani said, "Now we walk."

And they did. They walked through most of the city. Foggia is small enough that no one really needs a car. You can easily get from one end to the other by foot in less than two hours. They didn't have a destination in mind, from what Tera could tell. They just kept moving. Dott.ssa Giuliani would come to a fork in an alley and look at Tera.

"Now what?" Tera asked.

"You choose!" she would reply. It was strangely empowering. Tera enjoyed this kind of aimless wandering, and it was enjoyable to share this experience with someone as calming and down to earth as Fabrizia. Tera learned a few things about the city that she didn't know before. Some of the history of the buildings... some interesting gossip about the shopkeepers. There was a hidden path behind a movie theater that looked utterly impassable, but somehow they squeezed their way through. They stopped for Mediterranean food for lunch. All in all it was a fun journey, but the two of them noticed an unusual number of foreign faces near the neighborhood that housed the *Fiore Dorato*. Strange visitors walking the streets; curious parties with cameras and no smiles; tragedy tourists.

They made it back to the counseling center without Tera realizing it. She told Fabrizia that they needed a bigger sign on their door so people could find them more easily.

"I think you should come back tomorrow," she told Tera. "We will go for another walk. This will be good to do. Walking is good therapy."

Tera thanked her and upon Dott.ssa Giuliani's recommendation, canceled her evening music gig, spending most of the rest of the day in the Foggia University library, looking over the Italian CD selections. She found a corner under the library's impressive curved brick ceiling and sat with her eyes closed and headphones on. Corners were generally a toss-up for Tera. Sometimes they made her feel safe, while other times they made her feel, well, cornered. It helped to know that there was strict security to get into the university. There were no guns here. She felt a little safer.

Tera ate dinner alone. She watched an old Italian soap opera about the Carabinieri until she fell asleep. She woke up at three in the morning feeling sick. She drank some water and tried to fall back asleep, but she couldn't. She stared at a painting on her wall, depicting two paths in a wood. She thought about which road she would take if Fabrizia said, "You choose!"

8

Thursday.

Tera woke up suddenly to a loud pounding on her door. She was a little confused, although thankful to realize that she had gotten some sleep. She went to the door in her pajamas and unlatched all the locks but the chain. She opened the door a crack. There was nobody there. She took a step back and closed the door, undid the chain, and opened the door entirely. No one. Only the empty stairwell. She walked out and looked up and down the stairs. Nothing. This made her feel both stupid and paranoid.

She started packing her things. She needed to move. A quick search online and a few phone calls later and she found a nice, newer building, with vacancies on the first floor. It was still in the city, and had a similar price point. She could move there for the time being, and worry about moving out of Foggia another week.

She ate breakfast, staring at her quiet apartment. She thought about the restaurant shooter, and the money he gave her for his song request. She never told the cops about the money. Would it make any difference? They would probably just take the money away. She would rather spend it. She set her dishes by the sink, next to the other dishes by the sink. She walked into the front room and opened the piano lid.

Inside was the money from the shooter. It was seven-hundred Euros. Was this blood money? It didn't look different from other money. Was she hurting others by keeping this?

She showed up early to her appointment with Dott.ssa Giuliani, arriving a full hour ahead of schedule. She sat in the lobby of the counseling center and read some literature about "healing." She enjoyed seeing how Italy approached generic stock photos in their pamphlets. Even in Italian, most of the text on "moving forward" and "working through pain" sounded cliche to her. Where was the pamphlet called "How to get up in the morning," or "How to sleep at night?" She could use advice on both of those.

Today's session was different. They talked about the shooting. Sort of. Fabrizia had Tera write down words that described how she felt about what happened. She wrote them on notecards, and they laid them down on the floor. Tera wrote down words like "pointless," "haunting," "loud," "evil," "violent," "fast," "confusing," "exciting," and "sexy." She wasn't sure why she wrote down "sexy," but it came to her, so she wrote it down.

Fabrizia gave Tera photos to look at - more Italian stock photos - and told her to pick the one that she most identified with right now. She chose a picture of a rooftop below a mostly clear night sky. Fabrizia asked Tera why she chose that picture. Tera had looked at the other pictures. There were pictures of bikes, doors, objects, people, coffee, houses, flowers, nature, hands, fists, fire…

"I can't sleep at night," she said, and then began to recite: *"Resto a vegliare:sono come un passero solitario sopra il tetto. Tutto il giorno mi insultano i miei nemici, furenti imprecano contro di me."* She touched the photo, "Psalms one-o-two, eight and nine."

Later, whilst on their therapeutic stroll, the two women started the process of talking about the past. They didn't dive as deep as Fabrizia would have liked, but they spent a good amount of time talking about Tera's move to Italy, and her sleepless nights.

"Reality is easier when I'm tired," Tera mused.

"I have never heard someone say those words before." Fabrizia's intonation bounced through the English language like a tiny car on cobblestone, but her concern was steady, and her voice was calm. "Have you ever thought about getting a roommate?" she asked Tera.

"I'd prefer not to have one right now. Life is easier when you're alone."

Fabrizia hummed some tune for a minute.

"What is the worst thing," Dott.ssa Giuliani asked, "about being lonely?"

Tera thought about it.

"Probably that you get used to it…"

9

Thursday night was almost identical to Wednesday night. Tera wondered how many television shows it would take to wipe away the events of that week. Even the bad acting seemed more real than her own life.

10

Friday night.

The events of the day came and went and Tera still couldn't sleep. With most of the boxes now packed, the walls bare, and the space echoing memories of the last two years, it was all she could do to remain still on her bed. Mattress rather. The frame was packed up, so she was a few inches closer to the floor than usual. Her laptop was now plugged into the once overcrowded outlet by the bed, now that the desk was no longer there. Tonight she was streaming Korean dramas.

She picked up her phone. It was 1:22. Maria was probably still awake. She gave her a call.

"*Pronto...* Tera? Are you ok?"

"*Ciao Maria.* Yeah... I can't sleep."

Maria often worked at unusual times, since she was her own boss and could choose her hours. Late nights often brought the two of them together.

"Do you want to come over?" Maria asked.

"No... I'm not really interested in leaving my apartment right now... in the middle of the night... I would wake up your sisters. Besides, I don't want to get dressed." Tera was wearing her most comfortable tank-top and pajama shorts.

"Do you want me to come over there? I can come over now!" Maria set down a pencil on her desk and stood up. Her room was very tidy. Her desk lamp illuminated her cozy office-space in a calm yellow glow.

Tera's apartment was dark, lit only by the nightlight in the kitchen and her laptop, which created a blue atmosphere that was unsettling; angular shadows filled the walls behind all the stacked boxes, and blinked in the computer's changing light.

"No, that's alright. I think I just need to talk." Tera was lying on her back, watching the light from the computer dance on the ceiling. Maria had already walked out of her room, over to the front door of the house, and grabbed her coat.

"Oh, ok! I can do that." Maria put her coat back on the rack and sat down on a cotton-covered orange couch in her family's living room.

"I went to the police station again today," Tera started to say.

"That's right! You said you were going to do that. How did it go?" Maria asked excitedly.

"They wanted me to look at some photos, to see if I recognized the..." she paused, "a gun from the shooting."

"Wow! Did they find the killer, who got away?"

"Heh, no. And I'm afraid I wasn't much help to them today. I didn't recognize any of the... guns in the pictures. Although I did think that two of them looked familiar."

"Oh, I see. What does that mean? Do they know how they can catch the shooter?"

"I'm not sure about that. But hey, something else happened while I was there. I wanted your opinion."

"Yes?" Maria was very actively listening.

"When I was getting ready to leave the room, where they asked me all the questions, you know, to go back to the lobby and leave the station..."

Tera closed her eyes - her words sounded jumbled to her.

"...the police Sergeant was all like, 'hey if you remember anything else, give us a call.' But then he looked at me and said... he said 'you can call me anytime.' So, I thought - ok, I get it - But THEN, he said, 'if you need anything,' and I thought... that's a little odd. I mean, why was he saying all of that, you know?"

"Ohh," Maria said, after processing for a bit. "Mmm. I see." She was nodding at the upper corner of the living room.

"Earlier he had asked me how my therapy sessions were going, like he was so concerned about me, and I thought..."

"You think maybe he was flirting with you?" Maria opened her mouth wide and then closed it in a big smile. She then began to laugh. Tera waited a few seconds.

"Maybe?" She sounded skeptical, and a bit embarrassed. "It just seemed so... subtle..." Tera knew very well that in Italy, flirting is rarely subtle. "But maybe I'm wrong about it, you know? Maybe he just feels sorry for me because of what I've been through, with everything before, and now with this. He seemed pretty worried about me when they were questioning me again this morning. Like, maybe he's afraid I'm suicidal?" Tera sighed. "I'm afraid I'm..."

"Is he good looking?" Maria chimed in.

"What?"

"This man, is he good looking?"

"Hmm... yes," Tera said, reluctantly.

"Yes?!" Maria repeated back.

"Well, I mean, he's charming..."

"Do you like him?" Maria pressed.

"Maybe?" Tera admitted.

"Ahh," Maria said slowly. "This is VERY interesting, isn't it. Oh! Is he married?"

"That's a great question. I don't know." Although Tera was already thinking about all the clues she had on the Sergeant. No wedding ring. Able to get around quickly from home to work. Never mentioned any family. Only a photo of his parents in his office. Not that she was looking for these details, she just happened to remember them all very clearly. He was also taller than her, was right-handed, and had a nice smile. He seemed busy enough with his career, maybe he had never married.

"What?" Maria squeaked. "How old?"

Tera furrowed her brow. She hated trying to figure this stuff out by observation alone, but she knew why this detail was so important for Maria. There were enough old suitors in their life already. But Tera was typically pretty bad at guessing age; she thought Matteo was a teenager when they first met, and he never let it down. The cultural barrier didn't make it easier either.

"He's probably our age," Tera began, "but I don't know, he might be older, maybe thirty or forty." Tera grimaced. "Yikes," she added.

"Forty!" Maria shouted. "*Santo cielo*... Does he already have grey hairs?"

"Another good question..." Tera replied, more as a joke. She thought about the men at their church. She knew the Sergeant didn't have any grey hair yet.

"Tera!" Maria squeaked. Tera laughed.

"No, he actually has... light brown... I think you would call it... blonde hair?" Tera said.

"What? Is he foreign?"

"No... He's Italian... I don't know, Maria. Maybe he's forty, and half Swiss and..."

"Well, you know what it means," Maria interrupted, speaking slowly, and in a lower tone, "when a man is so old and has never married?" Tera said nothing. She was interested to see where Maria was going with this.

"It means something is wrong. He must have some terrible problem. Maybe, maybe he is a slob! Always leaving a mess!" Maria said excitedly. Tera laughed again.

"Or..." Maria continued. "Maybe he yells, and scares away all the women!"

"What?" Tera scoffed.

"Maybe he is too picky! No one is good enough for him, so he never marries. Oh!" Maria threw herself back on the couch. "You must be careful!" she said, in a hushed voice. "He will probably mislead you! He probably cannot commit! You will think he will propose, but he never will! You will date him forever, until YOU are forty, and then he will die of old age, before you ever get to marry him. *Ohibò...*" Maria then started to make that "tsk-tsk" sound with her tongue.

"Yep. I'm sure that's it." Tera covered her face with her free hand.

"Are his hairs really blonde?" Maria asked.

"Well, they're not black."

"Hmm..." Maria pondered. "What about his eyes?"

"He has two of them." Tera was ready for this to be done. Maria let out a playful "Grr..."

"So..." Tera moaned. "What do you think I should do?"

There was a long pause.

"Call him," Maria said quickly.

"What, now?"

"No, not now! Later. Tomorrow, maybe. Ask him to help you move. Tell him you need help. He said to call if you need anything, yes? Ask him and his brothers to help you move."

"He might not have any brothers, Maria."

"You will find out! Yes, I can see this. He will come over with all of his brothers, and you can find out then why he is not yet married. And who knows!" Maria sat up on her couch. "Maybe he has a younger brother who is better looking, with no grey hairs. Oh! And maybe he has TWO younger brothers, one for you, and one for me!"

This conversation was surely at its end. Tera thanked Maria for her "advice," and hung up the phone.

Tera had been hoping to get a confirmation of her own pitiful state, but, this is why she and Maria were friends. Maria always saw the brightest angle to any story, and had an odd way of making Tera feel better. And if Tera's suspicions were right about Sgt. Conti, then it was best to include Maria in this process. Honestly, Tera didn't know how to do this kind of thing anymore. Her heart had turned into an impenetrable box after her husband and sister were killed, and the very idea of moving on to a new relationship made her feel guilty, dirty, and nauseous.

Tera soon fell asleep, her mind full of emotionally chaotic music. She eventually landed in a dream. She was back in the States, with her older sister. They were looking at a house. A house that was also a car. There were wheels built into the sides of the structure, as if it were some kind of mobile-home on steroids. Her sister asked her if she remembered how to "drive one of these," and Tera replied, "only if you give me the keys!" to which her sister pulled out a single key on a ring, and handed it to her. But Tera dropped it, and it hit the ground with the sound of breaking glass, which woke Tera up.

11

Saturday.

But the sound of breaking glass wasn't a dream, was it? She opened her eyes and listened. Silence. She held her breath and remained still on her bed, her heart now beating fast. Her laptop screen had gone to sleep, and the room was dark. She strained to listen until she heard a quiet click. What was that? She sat up. Was this her imagination, or was there a reasonable explanation for this? She stayed still, listening to the sound of her breathing, heartbeat, and the weird hum of her central nervous system, buzzing louder and louder in her head the more she paid attention to it. Then she heard the muffled sound of her kitchen window slowly slide open.

Adrenalin flooded her body, and before she had time to think, she found she had quietly slid off the mattress, grabbed her gun from under her pillow, and tiptoed into the front room, positioning herself next to the kitchen doorway. She knew what she would do. The intruder would walk through the doorway, and if they had a weapon, she would fire. If they didn't, she would start yelling, and threaten them out of her apartment. Then, after either shooting them, or after the intruder was gone, she would call the police.

She waited, her back against the wall. The room was cluttered with stacks of boxes, hardly visible in the dark but for the kitchen nightlight and some indirect street light reflecting off the neighboring buildings through the windows. She listened... but heard nothing.

Earlier at the police station, she did exactly what the guy in the salon had told her to do. She didn't identify the shooter from the photos. She didn't even narrow it down for them. And she only gave her best guess at the gun, since she honestly couldn't tell a Walther from a Remington. So why would this be happening?

She adjusted the grip on her gun. She knew how to hold it. She used to go to shooting ranges back in the States. It helped her feel powerful to know how to shoot. And though it was times like this that she had prepared for, she never thought it would actually happen again. She waited. Every second felt like an eternity as she waited.

"I have a question for you." The deep voice came from the kitchen. Tera's heart skipped a beat. It was unmistakably that of the restaurant shooter. Tera swallowed. She had seen this man fight, and she was no match. So much for plan A.

"Get out of my apartment," she mumbled, probably too quickly. She was frightened at the sound of her voice. She had envisioned a threatening tone, but what had come out was nothing more than the sound of a scared young woman. She felt embarrassed. Which made her mad. This increased her focus. She quietly lowered the magazine out of her gun and set it behind a box stacked next to her. She didn't want to get killed with her own gun. This reminded her of chess, and she was planning for the long game now.

"You chose not to identify me." His voice was close. He was leaning against the other side of the wall in the kitchen. They were back to back.

"I'd like to know why," he said.

Tera was thinking through her options. She could try to fight him, or try to run. Or she could talk to him. At this point, she didn't even know if he had a weapon.

"If that's all you wanted to know…" she started, trying to sound more confident, "You could have called, and spared breaking my window." She wanted to add "I have to pay a deposit on that," but decided the fewer words, the better. She looked around the room. Why couldn't she have moved yesterday? Amidst the boxes she spotted her sword near the piano. It was a decorative sword from Thailand. It probably wasn't even sharp. But next to it was her knife from Kenya. She had been using it to cut boxes. It was very sharp.

"You're a bit of an enigma, aren't you?" he said playfully, in what now seemed to Tera to be an unmistakably British accent. He started to turn his body, shifting his weight, causing the floor to creak. Tera started to turn towards the doorway, with her gun raised. He moved quickly through the doorway, Tera stepping back towards the piano, her gun aimed at his head.

"I just figured," she said, inching slowly back, "that you didn't want the world to see you."

The man quickly closed the distance between the two of them and swung his arm under Tera's, gaining control of her hands. She fought to keep hold of the gun, but he was much stronger than she was. He had the gun out of her grip in less than a second, but then he just stood there, seemingly uninterested in hurting her. He looked slightly amused.

She reached for the knife, accidentally knocking it to the ground by the door. In a fluster, she grabbed the sword. She flung off the decorative dragon scabbard which hit the floor with a crash. Entertained, the man held the gun low with his right hand, and slowly stepped back; she had the point of her katana pressing in his face, forcing him to withdraw toward the kitchen.

She lunged forward and twisted the blade with an upward motion, surprising even herself as she cut the underside of the man's left arm. He grimaced, and sharply pulled back his arm. It had been years since she had studied kendo, and she was sure that this bought of luck was more muscle memory than skill. But it was a short-lived victory, as the man easily took advantage of the blade's vertical position and charged forward, pinning Tera's arms and sword, pushing her body into the front wall, her gun pointed in her stomach.

Both parties took this opportunity to breathe. There was now a delicate balance of tensions at play, as Tera was currently pushing back against the man's right hand, to keep her katana blade from cutting her arm and face. His right arm was crossing his body, pinning her arms to the wall with his weight, his right hand fighting for control of the sword's hilt. His right leg pinned her left. His left hand now had the gun. Weighing her options, and considering the gun wasn't loaded, she lifted both legs into the air, allowing her body weight to bring the sword, and herself, to the floor with a loud thud, the man stumbling back. She reached for the nearby knife and heard the gun trigger click.

"Good night!" she exclaimed in astonishment, as she rushed the man who was puzzling at the gun, back into some boxes, her left hand grabbing his black shirt, with her right hand pushing the blade of the knife with a reverse grip against the side of his inner thigh.

"You really would have shot me?!"

"That's clever. You're a little smarter than you look," he commented, dropping the gun, laughing a bit.

"What's that supposed to mean?!" she yelled back, pressing the blade closer. He let her guide him out of the living room, back into the kitchen. He stepped back towards the broken window and raised both hands, with some small amounts of blood dripping down his arm onto the rest of his clothes.

"Get the hell out!" she yelled, holding tightly to the knife. The man straightened up and brushed himself off. Looking at Tera, he lifted his left arm and motioned to the bleeding cut,

"Ouch," he said coolly, before lowering his arm back to his side. He appeared unphased, but maybe a bit annoyed.

He slowly looked her over, as if trying to understand. Tera remained angry and determined, breathing heavily.

"Why are you protecting me?" he asked. Tera gathered her wits.

"Because I value my own life. Your friends aren't very nice."

"Are you a friend?" he asked.

She responded with a slight pause between words, "I'd prefer not to be involved."

The sound of quick, heavy footsteps sounded through the wall, and then a loud pounding on Tera's door.

"Good luck with that," he said quietly, now looking bothered. "If you truly value your life, you'll keep this little meeting a secret. I hope you can take care of yourself." He raised both eyebrows at her, before leaping over the dirty dishes and climbing out the window.

"Tera! Tera? *Stai bene? Oddio...*" It was Sig.ra. Bianchi, the upstairs landlady. Tera walked over to the front room, her eyes still on the kitchen window. Leaving the door chain in place, she unlocked the bolt and opened the door a crack, holding the knife behind her back with her left hand.

"*Sì?*" Tera said, quietly.

"Tera! *Che cosa sta succedendo, sei in pericolo? Oddio, oddio!*" She was wearing a long floral nightgown and had her hair in curlers. She looked very distressed.

"It's ok, *Signora* Bianchi, *sto bene, sto bene.*" Tera tried to speak in a calm voice.

"Did I wake you up?"

"*Ho sentito i rumori e ho chiamato la polizia...*"

"What?!" Tera began to panic.

12

She shut the door slowly on Sig.ra. Bianchi, who kept on asking questions through the door in excitement and worry. If Sig.ra. Bianchi called the police, then Tera only had minutes to get her story together. She wasn't about to tell them that the "killer at large" showed up, at HER place, to ask her why she was LYING to the police; any connection with that man made her look incredibly suspicious, and he didn't offer much encouragement with his parting words. If they found out he was there, it would end up in the news.

She turned on the lights. She looked around. She put the knife in a box by the piano. She ran to the kitchen, grabbed a sponge from out of the sink. Having used up all the dish soap yesterday, and being unsure where her cleaning supplies were packed, she wet the sponge with water and began scrubbing around anywhere she could find blood. The trail was pretty easy to track: a clear line from the kitchen window along the tile floor to the sword in the front room. There wasn't a large volume of blood, but she seemed to keep seeing traces of it, wherever she looked. A teeny dark dot would turn into a big pink blur after she tried to mop it up, causing her anxiety to rise. She took a deep breath. This was going to require more time than she had.

She could clearly hear police sirens in the distance through the open window. It wouldn't be long before they wound their way through the maze of skinny streets to her door. She reached up and closed the large, aged window, and looked at the thin, old, broken glass. It had obviously been broken in from the outside; bits and shards still sprinkled the countertop.

She locked the window, rushed back to the front room, and grabbed the katana. She brought the sword into the kitchen and, after a moment of reconsidering, stabbed the remaining glass in the window - throwing more pieces onto the counter, some falling passed the outside ledge and onto the neighbor's little balcony below.

She carefully set down the sword and picked up a piece of the foggy-tinted glass. She climbed onto the counter by the window. She held her right foot in one hand, and the sharp piece of glass in the other. She didn't have time to clean up all the blood. She would need an explanation. Her palms started sweating and her breathing quickened; she knew what she had to do.

Quickly, before she could let herself think about it, she cut into the ball of her foot with the jagged piece of glass. It stung harshly and her hand recoiled from the pain, dropping the bloody glass shard on the floor. Tera swore, and barefoot, carefully ran back to the bedroom. Her foot was bleeding more than she expected. Desperately trying not to panic, she took a piece of packing tape and wrapped it around her foot. The sirens were now outside the building.

She turned on her computer. Her computer had stopped streaming at the beginning of an episode of that Korean drama. "Are you still watching?" it read, on the screen. She heard the sirens stop. Car doors being shut. Sig.ra. Bianchi was now hurrying down the stairs. Tera quickly ran back to the front room and looked around. She grabbed the gun, the magazine, and the sword scabbard. She put the scabbard back by the sword stand, and ran the gun back to her bedroom pillow, just as the police could be heard loudly running up the stairs.

Starting to shake in panic, she ran into the bathroom, turned on the sink, and started washing her hands. She looked in the mirror at herself. Was she covered in blood? Was she visibly hurt? What she saw truly surprised her. Apart from the shaking, she saw a strong looking woman, serious and determined, with the ability to push through exhaustion and trauma when her life depended on it. The adrenaline high that had been supporting her through the last ten minutes was now all but spent, and hysteria was beginning to gain full control of her body. She heard the Police break through the door.

"*Pronto! Polizia!*"

"*Signorina?*"

"*Polizia!*"

She quickly splashed water on her face and called back to them. She wiped her face with the bath towel and slowly collapsed to the floor, holding her knees, trembling uncontrollably. She looked through the door and saw two of

Italy's finest, *la Polizia di Stato*, standing in her bedroom. It wasn't hard for her to pretend to be embarrassed, since she was still in her pajamas, and currently fighting a panic attack.

"Hi," she waved from the floor, trying to stop shaking. She tried to smile, and spoke nervously, "everything is ok, there is no emergency." One of the policemen, upon seeing her, started to speak into a radio through an earpiece. Tera recognized him. He was the scraggly police agent from the station. Tera overheard him report *"la donna del ristorante è ancora qui."* She knew what that meant. It meant that Sgt. Conti was soon coming over too, to see her in her pajamas.

"No, no, no!" She started to crawl out of the bathroom towards them, and wobbling, stood up. She put her hands out, waving frantically.

"There is nothing wrong. You can leave, you can ALL," she watched as a third police agent began to move boxes and open cabinets, "LEAVE. PLEASE." She steadied herself against the wall, still trembling, and very worried.

"La finestra...?" the third agent called out from the kitchen. Tera could see Sig.ra. Bianchi outside the door, speaking rapidly to a fourth police agent, who was jotting down notes on her notepad. Sig.ra. Bianchi was telling her that there was a loud crash, sounds of a struggle, and distressed shouts. She told her that she heard the voice of a man. Tera tried to stop her landlady from saying more, pleading with her that she was alright and that this was a

misunderstanding. Tera repeatedly told the police that there was no emergency and that they didn't need to be there.

"What happened, Miss?" asked agent Ferraro, a middle aged policeman with pretty eyes. Tera was now feeling very overwhelmed.

"Why is your window broken? Why did your neighbor call us for an emergency?" Tera breathed heavily and quickly, trying to control herself enough to speak.

"Mrs. Bianchi called because she is a good neighbor," Tera had to fight to keep herself from crying. She hated crying. Made her feel weak. So she fought it back, with anger. Lots of anger. Her body stopped shaking. She faced the police agent with confidence.

"I broke my window," she motioned toward the kitchen, *"and I was upset, and that woke up my neighbors,"* she looked out at Sig.ra. Bianchi and called out, *"Mi dispiace!"*

"How did you break the window?"

Tera turned back to the agent,

"With my, uh, with my sword."

She brought her left hand up to her head and started to push her hair around.

"Spada?" Ferraro repeated, puzzled. The scraggly cop confirmed from the kitchen that there was a sword on the ground.

"Why did you do this?" Ferraro asked. Tera shifted her weight off from her cut foot, which was pulsing in pain. She wanted to scream but kept her focus. She took her time.

"Um... I didn't want to. It was an accident. I was watching a TV show..." she motioned over to her laptop, *"They were sword fighting on the show..."* Tera's face started to turn red with embarrassment. This sounded pretty stupid. The scraggly cop shouted over, *"C'è sangue sul pavimento."* He pointed to the spots of blood on the floor. Tera nodded and showed *Agente* Ferraro her foot.

"Yeah, watch your step! Oh *mannaggia a me...*" She winced and sat down on the piano bench, holding her right heel. She slowly set her foot down and put her face in her hands. Scraggle-cop said some more things into his earpiece. The agent in the stairwell continued to ask questions of Sig.ra. Bianchi, and Sig.ra. Gabrielli, who had now joined. It wouldn't be long before Sig. Lombardo would stick his head out of his door too. Ferraro looked at Tera.

"We were told there was shouting," he said, calmly.

"*Sì...*" Tera was still holding her head. *"That was me. I was upset about my foot."*

"And sounds of a struggle? Pounding on the walls?" he inquired.

"That was me..." she was almost moaning. *"I was..."* she sighed, *"Angry. I'm so sorry. This is all so embarrassing. I don't mean to waste your time like this. I've just been going through a lot."*

More sirens could be heard outside the apartment building. Tera looked up at Ferraro, who was nodding at her sympathetically. Scraggy walked over and gave *Agente* Ferraro a quick pat on the shoulder, then headed out of the tiny apartment into the stairwell with the other police agents.

*"And the voice of the man?"*Ferraro asked Tera. She
pointed into the bedroom. The agent walked to the doorway
and peered in. The computer was paused on the Korean
drama. He lifted his cap and scratched his head. "Ok..." he
said slowly. With his police cap lifted, signs of heavy
bruising revealed themselves on the side of his head and
neck. All at once, Tera realized that Ferraro had been one of
the first to arrive at the *Fiore Dorato* after the shooting. Tera
couldn't help but feel disturbed, thinking about how his
bruises were connected to the sweat on her neck. The
shadow that hung over her probably also hung over him. She
remained on the piano bench, her head whirling, starting to
feel a little sick.

Ferraro walked over to the front door and spoke
softly to Scraggy, who was nodding. There was a sound of
two more car doors slamming shut, and it took only a few
seconds before *Sovrintendente* Conti was standing in the
apartment doorway, listening to three agents talk over each
other, but keeping his eyes on Tera, who despite her best
efforts to stare into the floor, could only see his eyes on her.
She felt that she might break apart, but did her best to hold
herself together.

Moments later a man and woman in slightly different
uniforms pushed through the crowded stairwell and started to
move slowly through the apartment, setting down equipment,
and putting on blue plastic gloves. Tera's eyes opened wide
at this. One of them started taking pictures.

"What are you doing?!" She jumped up from the piano bench, ready to forcefully shove everyone out.

"Tera?" It was the Sergeant. She couldn't look him in the face, so she looked at his shoulder. Her face again turned bright red, her stomach in knots.

"I'm sorry," she said. "You don't need to be here for this."

They stood there for a long moment before he slowly escorted her out of the apartment, placing his police jacket over her bare shoulders as they walked down to the police cars. Before he led her out, Tera saw the woman with blue gloves open her bathroom mirror and examine her toothpaste; the man with blue gloves picked up glass and put it in a bag. She was so thankful that she had already taken out her trash and cleaned the bathroom.

Tera sat in the Sergeant's Alfa Romeo, watching as what looked like the entire Carabinieri Specialist Units Division moved through the apartment, no doubt investigating all of her personal things. Scraggy and Ferraro drove off and were soon replaced with *Tenente* Napolitano, who didn't stay long. Every five minutes someone new showed up. She waited for *Sovrintendente* Conti to return to the car and drive her back to the police station, but he remained in the building's lobby, conferring with others. They bandaged her foot properly and brought her a blanket and some water. She told her story fifty times to ten different people, each time believing it more and more. She broke her window. She bled on the floor. She yelled at herself.

An hour passed, and eventually everyone left, except for the neighbors and the Sergeant. Tera watched with a sense of hopelessness in her eyes as the forensics team walked off with her laptop. No more Netflix. The sky was beginning to show signs of daybreak, and Tera was ready to break down again. *Sovrintendente* Conti returned to the car and brought Tera back up to her apartment. For the most part, things looked the same. Stacks of boxes randomly placed throughout the rooms. Her dirty dishes were still there. The Sergeant took a final look at Tera before bidding the apartment tenants goodbye and getting the heck out.

The door's latch was broken, so there was no closing it. There was a draft from the broken window, and the apartment had cooled off. Tera put her hands on the kitchen counter and looked out the broken window. All the glass had been swept up by the forensics team. She stretched herself out and stuck her head through the empty pane. She looked down at the lower balcony, now also cleaned off. On the ground below she saw Sgt. Conti talking to another man outside the front door. They both eventually got into the last police car and drove away, eastward.

"Hey," Tera said quietly to herself, while she watched the blue car fade into the sunrise. "Want to help me move?"

13

Tera pushed a box in front of the busted door to keep it from swinging open-and-closed in the draft from the window. She walked back to her bedroom and threw herself onto the mattress, using what energy was left to cry into her pillow. After some amount of time had passed, she woke up, to hear her phone ringing in the other room.

"No," she said, to the phone, which rang four more times before going to voicemail. She started to drift off to sleep again before waking up to the "ding" that indicates someone has left a message. Tera groaned pitifully into her pillow before forcing her way out of bed, over to her phone. She picked it up. It was an unknown number. Bringing the phone back with her she once again threw herself onto the bed, facedown. She started the voicemail.

"Thought you'd want to know..." It was the voice of the restaurant shooter. "...they took your bloody sponge." The recording clicked abruptly to an end.

"I hate you," Tera muttered, before pushing her phone calmly off the bed onto the floor. After a minute she quickly snatched it back and deleted the voicemail.

She thought about it. What would happen if the police tested "the bloody sponge" and found remains of the shooter's blood? Did they have any DNA from *Fiore Dorato* to compare it to? There was far too much law enforcement in her apartment last night - they had to have suspected that the shooter was there. If they tested the sponge, they would know she was lying, and they would know he was there. They would probably interrogate her again. Even if she told them everything she knew, she would probably still end up either dead, or in Italian prison. She definitely didn't want to go to Italian prison. Being dead didn't seem so bad right now.

She slumped over the bed and looked at her phone again - It was 10:42 in the morning. How was she supposed to stop them from testing the blood in the sponge? It's not like she had any close connections with any members of the police force with any amount of power to do anything about it.

She blinked at her reflection in the phone. She sat up, rubbing her face with her hand. She didn't have time to be shy; she dialed Conti's number.

"*Pronto*," he answered immediately, which caught her off guard.

"Hi!" she said, surprised. "It's Tera. Um, everything is fine. I… was… just wondering…" She felt very awkward about this. "Are you busy right now?" she asked, nervously.

"Why do you ask?"

"You know what," she said quickly, "don't worry about it, I don't know why I called. You're probably working."

"Nonononono... what is it? What do you need?"

About an hour later he showed up with three other men and a small cargo truck. He called up to her apartment from the street, with a whistle through his teeth. She hobbled over to the barred window in the front room, to see him waving up at her. It was strange to see him out of his uniform, no hat, no gun. He was wearing a short-sleeved, button-down white shirt, and baggy grey cargo shorts. The others were dressed just as casually, two men leaning against the truck bed, one lighting a cigarette. The side of the vehicle read *"Formaggio di Foggia."* The truck was blocking traffic in the narrow one-way street outside the building, so they got to work right away.

With the five of them it took little time to get everything out of the apartment. Even after two years of accumulating stuff, Tera still didn't own much. Most of her boxes were full of furniture parts, artwork, books, and sheet music. Lots and lots of sheet music. The piano was a bit of a miracle, but the four men made it down the three flights of stairs somehow. When all was said and done, the truck remained only half full.

Tera recognized one of the men from the police station, from the first questioning. She was pretty sure he was the Sgt. Chief. Few words were exchanged between any of them until after the apartment was emptied out, so she didn't bother bringing it up.

"Grazie per l'aiuto," she thanked the men.

"Sergente," she nodded.

"Luca," he smiled. "Please."

"*Grazie, Luca.*" She looked at the others. "So who are you guys?"

They laughed. The older, familiar policeman went first.

"Alfredo," he nodded. The other two men were poking each other. The shorter one, with green-tinted sunglasses, chimed in.

"We are both called Marco," he laughed, and reached out his hand. "*Marco Moretti, piacere di conoscerla.*"

Tera shook his hand, but he pulled her in for a friendly hug. He smelled like smoke, but Tera tried to be polite about it.

"*Un altro Marco,*" said the taller, scruffy one, who also laughed before giving her a brief hug.

"*Lei dove si sta trasferrendo?*" asked Marco Moretti. They all looked at Tera, who showed them a map on her phone.

"Oh, hang on a minute," Tera said, handing the Sergeant her phone, "*Ho dimenticato,*" and she trotted back to the apartment, limping slightly as her foot still stung. She made it up the full four flights, to the door of Sig.ra. Bianchi. She knocked a few times before the tired-looking woman came to the door. Tera handed her the key, but Sig.ra. Bianchi pulled Tera into the apartment, while talking about everything. Tera refused to say anything about the shooting or the incident last night, and Sig.ra. Bianchi eventually let it go, but not without keeping a suspicion about her.

Bianchi had some papers for Tera to sign, but wouldn't let her touch them until she ate something. She wouldn't take the money Tera offered for her front door, but she did take the fee for the window. She hugged her and laughed. She cried, and told her to get married. Tried setting her up with her best friend's grandsons. Tera eventually got out of there by telling Sig.ra. Bianchi that four men were already waiting for her down by the road. This might have been a mistake, because as soon as she said this, Sig.ra. Bianchi put on her shoes, and together they walked down the four flights to meet Tera's prospects. But when they got there it was only Luca Conti, leaning against the wall in the lobby.

"*Salve*," he greeted the older woman. She must have not recognized him out of uniform; she kissed his cheeks in greeting, took his arm, and asked him questions about his health, his mother, and his work.

"Where are the others?" Tera interrupted her land lady's interview. Luca, still holding Sig.ra. Bianchi's hand, looked at Tera.

"Well, I figured they should go on ahead. I drove separately, so we can catch up... whenever." This was working out well, Tera thought.

While she had some concern for that cheese truck - full of strangers - driving around with her whole apartment inside, she had far more concern for that confiscated sponge. Every minute she wondered if she was already too late.

14

For some reason she expected to be riding in a police car, so she was rather delighted to see his black Audi parked out front. Luca opened the door for her, and she bid Sig.ra. Bianchi goodbye as they climbed in and drove off.

It was a bit intimidating, riding next to him. Tera wasn't sure where to look. She was a bit too cowardly to look him in the face, but since he was driving, he couldn't exactly stare back, so it made for a good opportunity to see if he had any gray hair.

Her mind was pouring over strategies to get them to wherever the forensics team ended up. But she couldn't bring that up point-blank, at least not without discussing other unwanted topics. She had to start with the basics (whatever those were) and work her way up to forensics. Luca was already helping her move, which was a big favor. She wasn't sure how to ask him for another, bigger one. An illegal one. A go-to-Italian-prison one. But she didn't have to think too long about what to say, because he broke the ice.

"How long have you lived in that building?" he asked her.

"Shortly after I moved to Foggia. About two years ago."

"You could choose anywhere in Italy to live, and you came to Foggia? Why?" He laughed.

"I don't know…" Tera furrowed her brow, "I like how… simple it is here. It's not overrun with tourists. It kind of reminds me of a pretty Lansing."

"Lansing?"

"That's a city back home." She felt nervous answering his questions. But this wasn't an interrogation, so she could ask back. "Do you live around here?"

"Mmhmm," he nodded.

"That's nice," she said after a while. They drove two more blocks in awkward silence. Tera looked out at the beautiful architecture as they rode. She didn't often ride in a car.

"So, you play the piano…" he started, breaking the tension. "Your neighbors told me that you are very good at it. They were sorry to hear you are moving."

Tera hadn't given much thought to her move. She had viewed that apartment as a temporary home, not wanting to be pinned down anywhere she couldn't leave on short notice. She appreciated that her neighbors didn't complain about her playing. She would miss that about them.

"How long have you been a cop?" she asked, still staring out the window at the buildings. He made four clicking sounds with his tongue while he thought,

"Fourteen years." He raised his right eyebrow as he pondered this.

"Have you always been a Sergeant?" she asked. He looked at her briefly, while they stopped at a light. But she didn't notice. She was captivated by the ornate windows of the building next to them.

"*Mah, no,*" he said. "*Ero nelle forze...per quattro anni, e...*"

"What division?" Tera interrupted.

"*Mah...* How do you say, Airplane Military?"

"Airforce..."

"*Sì.* Air Force. Then I was... *agente per quattro anni...* becoming *Vice Sovrintendente*, how you say, 'Vice Sergeant,' for five years. I've been Sovrintendente now... *per due anni.* Two years."

Tera always wondered if people knew when they were switching between languages like that. She sometimes caught herself doing it while translating English for Italian speakers.

"Is that where you learned to speak English?" she asked.

"No, it was my mother, who wanted us to learn English. She rightly believed we would get better jobs... so I took lessons when I was very young. But," he paused as he thought about the past, "there were times in the military where we would learn other languages. I also speak some Neapolitan and *Tedesco.*"

"Tedesco?"

"Ja... Ich spreche Deutsch."

"Oh, you mean German."

"Is that how you say it in English? *Sì*, German. Ah...
È simile a 'germano,' hmm." He mulled this over for a bit.
"When did you learn to speak Italian?"

"High school," she cringed. "Voice lessons. But I fell
in love with the language pretty quickly. How old were you,
when you joined the Italian Armed Forces?"

Luca looked quickly between Tera and the road, and
his face lit up with a smile.

"So young... I was eighteen years old," he smiled
big, "that was a long time ago."

"Do you enjoy your job?" She stopped looking out
the side window and started looking at the road in front of
them.

"I do... I enjoy helping people," he said. "Except,
sometimes it is not a fun job to do. Is this it?" He pointed at a
newer looking building as they drove past.

"That's it," she said. "I think we can pull around in
the back."

They quickly identified the others in the limited
parking area, both Marcos sitting on top of the truck,
throwing apples at each other. Alfredo was sitting in the
driver's seat, adjusting his glasses to look down at his phone.
They pulled up and parked next to them, Luca leaping out of
the car, quickly running around the back to open Tera's door
for her, but she beat him to it - leaving him standing there, to
put his thumbs in his pockets with a bothered grin.

Moving in was a little slower than moving out
because they spent most of this time talking to each other.

Whereas the old apartment had an old echoing stairwell, the new one had long, quiet hallways. Tera learned that "the second" Marco was a graphic designer and web developer. "Regular" Marco, or "smoker Marco" as Tera thought of him, works as an electrician, and also sells cheese with his family.

Tera didn't talk much to Alfredo, except for, *put that box over there,* "or, *"Thank you, yes"* and *"Thank you, no."* He never spoke in English and seemed wary of getting friendly with Tera. Made sense to her. She felt very strange about having two police Sergeants help her out. It felt like they were breaking some sort of protocol.

With everything moved in, they headed out together for a late lunch. Tera sat between Marco and Marco in a booth at the pizza restaurant. She liked these guys. Alfredo stayed up at the register for a while, even after they got their food, talking to the man behind the counter. Luca sat across from the three of them, amusingly isolated, turning to check on Alfredo every now and then. They ate and talked about the most random topics, occasionally drawing participation from the other patrons sitting nearby.

At one point, Luca mentioned to Tera that the Second Marco's obsessions were unrivaled. Second Marco apparently knew a lot about volcanoes and was very excited to tell everyone what he knew. Amidst his rambling, Tera wondered if Maria could find any use in her life for a scruffy graphic designer, so she interjected herself into his Vesuvius lecture to ask him if he was Catholic. He said yes, so she let it go. Unphased, Second Marco continued.

Alfredo eventually joined them for a few bites at the end. Marco Moretti insisted on paying for Tera's food, bickering with the other Marco for this honor at the register. Tera had greatly desired to pay for the four of them as a thank you, but the bill had already been settled by Alfredo, who wisely kept his distance.

On the way out the door, Luca stopped to talk to Tera. He said he wanted to know how she was doing. The others rode off in the empty truck while the two of them continued to talk in the doorway. A restaurant worker loomed nearby, pressuring them to leave so they could close up shop for their *riposo*. Luca hurriedly purchased two drinks to go, and they sat down at an outdoor table. Cathedral bells chimed somewhere nearby, and they watched the streets grow quiet around them as the city paused its activity for an afternoon siesta. After a few minutes, they settled back into conversation.

They talked about many things before Tera felt pressure to push the discussion towards her topics of interest. "So… Luca…" She blinked at him, thinking of what to say. He stared at her. "Maria, his eyes are brown," she thought, staring back into his gaze.

"Do you feel naked without your gun?" she asked.

He gave her a knowing look. He leaned slightly to his left and artfully lifted the right side of his shirt for a second, revealing a black handle tucked into a holster that wrapped around his waist. "Oh," she murmured.

"The answer is yes," he said, candidly. She hid her embarrassment behind a sip of her Coke. He glanced upward and smiled.

"I was rather charmed when you called me this morning," he looked over at the sunlit streets. "I figured you wouldn't want to talk to me after the events of last night. You seemed to be having a hard time." He looked back at her, concerned.

"Well…" Tera said, annoyed, "Yeah…"
She drank more of her Coke and looked around in a dodgy manner. "I still feel like an idiot. But you're being very nice about it all. And, for what it's worth," she looked at Luca, "I was going to ask you for help with moving anyway. So, there's that."

"Your neighbors," Luca said, trying to sound like a friend more than a policeman, "said that you never shout or yell."

Tera looked at the table for a minute.

"Luca," she began, "do you believe in ghosts?" She looked up at him. He scratched his head.

"Ghosts?"

"Yeah. I feel like I'm being haunted by my past, like…" she waved her hands, "like a ghost." She picked up a napkin and started folding it in odd ways.

"Like no matter where I am, I feel like I'm being watched, or like someone is following me." Luca seemed to understand this.

"And I can't sleep at night, because I keep seeing faces in the dark, or guns going off..."
She tore the napkin somewhat. "I can't even tell you," she said, looking at Luca, "How many things in this world sound like gunshots. They're everywhere. Just, just everywhere." Luca nodded.

"And no offense to you, or the good, good men at your police station," she picked up the napkin, continuing to pick at it, "but I kinda freak out every time I hear a siren, or see anyone in a uniform. And I really, really..." she bunched up the napkin into a compact little ball, "really don't like being interrogated." Luca didn't say anything but continued to watch Tera smoosh the napkin into the table.

"Do you know," she didn't look hopeful, "if you're any closer to catching that... guy?"

"The shooter?" Luca raised his eyebrows. "Today is my day off, you know." He took a drink of his soda. "Unfortunately, we have very little information about the man, apart from your testimony." Luca sounded like a cop when he said this.

"Was the forensics team able to find any DNA of the shooter at the scene?" Tera asked.

He shook his head slowly and looked reticent. "There is still a lot of material to go through. There are forensic teams from Lucera, Borgo Celano, Cerignola… A lot are involved."

Tera felt tremendous relief. But this wasn't over for her yet.

"Are you working with a forensics team in Foggia?"

"Of course. Well, personally I am not. Forensics is part of the Carabinieri, run by the military, not by the State." He took another drink of his soda and shrugged. "*Mah*… There would be no reason to limit this investigation to the teams in Foggia. Garbanzo had a history in multiple regions in Apulia."

"He had such a silly name…"

"But he was no laughing matter," Luca cut in, "He was brutal. Most certainly responsible for many violent deaths. You know why they called him 'Garbanzo?'"

Tera shook her head.

"Garbanzo is another word for *ceci*, or chickpea. His men smuggled…" Luca waved his hands over the table, "*cocaina,* the drug, through bean farms, all through Italy. He was working closely with dangerous individuals in underground drug trades. Very difficult to track him down. It's almost a relief to know that he is out of the picture now. Makes things a little easier for the GdF."

The GdF were the *Guardia di Finanza.* Tera had forgotten about them. Yet another division of Italian law enforcement. She looked shyly to the side.

"How closely do you work with the Carabinieri on cases like this?"

Luca looked bothered, "We don't normally have cases like this one, Tera. It's very unusual to have gang violence on this scale in our city." He looked at her, "The last homicide inside the city of Foggia was almost a year ago - this is usually a peaceful place. I'm used to dealing with theft, and fist-fights, and passports."

"Oh…" Tera said, again feeling quite embarrassed. "So you don't ever go to a forensics lab?"

"Occasionally," he said, "But they normally work directly with our superiors."

This was good to know.

"Why are you asking this?" Luca looked a little cautious.

"Well..." she looked evasive. She thought quickly. "They took my laptop. And I would really like that back."

"Mmm..." Luca nodded. "You will probably get that back."

"Makes me wonder what other things of mine they took, you know?" Tera was afraid to push the topic further without sounding suspicious. She put her hands in her pockets.

"We should talk about something else," she said.

Luca looked at her slyly and started to smile. "Ok," he admired her. "I like your hairs. This looks very good on you."

"Luca," Tera was suddenly distracted; mild alarm causing her to sit up sharply, "do you still have my phone?"

She would have said "thank you," but didn't care much what he thought about "her hairs" in light of her empty pockets. He shifted in his seat and looked a bit mischievous.

"Oh, you wanted this back?" he took her phone out of his coat pocket and slid it across the table to her.

"For a minute there I thought I lost it..." she picked it up.

"Maria called," Luca looked smug. "I told her you would call her back."

Tera looked at Luca, horrified. She quickly looked at her call history. Maria called alright, and they talked for two minutes. Maria could say a lot in two minutes. Tera sat still, blinking at her phone, trying not to think about it. Then Tera noticed that the number from the shooter was still in her call history. She looked up at Luca, who was still smiling.

"Do you know how to trace calls?" she asked slowly.

"*Certo*," he nodded.

"I got a call this morning from a strange number," she showed him her phone. He looked at it for a moment.

"Did you try calling them back?" He looked at her.

"No..." she said, "I'm... afraid to do that."

Luca finished his drink, then looked up the number in an app on his phone.

"This is unusual," he said after a minute. "Do you know anyone who might have called you from *Roma*? From a payphone?"

Tera looked uncomfortably to the side. Apparently she did, but she wasn't about to admit that.

"No names come to mind," she said, quite honestly. Luca looked at her phone again and typed in some more information to his app. She waited while he scrolled through some of the data.

"Hmm..." he said. "It looks like it was forwarded... through that payphone, from an unknown source. So it could have been anybody... *che strano*... My guess is that it was someone trying to sell you something."

Tera nodded.

"If you like," he went on to say, "I can look into it some more when I'm back at work."

"When do you have to go back to work?"

"Tomorrow. In the morning. Technically I'm on call right now." He gave her the phone. "I think," he smirked at her, "you should stop by and visit me at work some time. Then I can keep answering more of your questions."

She looked at him, concerned and embarrassed over what Maria might have said. Tera looked at the time on her phone in disbelief. Somehow they had been talking outside that restaurant for almost three hours.

"Oh no!" Her eyes were wide with wonder, but she kept a smile in her tone. "I have a gig in less than an hour, I need to go!"

"What do you have?" Luca asked, not understanding.

"A gig...*Il mio lavoro, suono il pianoforte.*" She stood up and looked at Luca. "Could you drop me off? It's north of the train tracks, I don't think I can walk there in time."

"Drop you?" Luca got up, nodded, and took out his keys as they walked down the sidewalk together. He looked at her hopefully, "May I... stay? Hear you play?"

15

It doesn't seem to matter what country you are in - all recording studios maintain the same two goals: relax the performers, and get the best sound possible. This small recording studio was the perfect healing atmosphere for Tera. It was a place to be creative, to express one's skills, to push yourself, and either spend or earn lots of money in a few hours.

Tera settled in right away with the dim lights, tranquil decor, and cozy furniture. From outside this place looked like an abandoned building, but inside was a truly welcoming environment. The other musicians looked familiar, but they didn't waste any time with chit chat; they were all here to make beautiful music... on a tight timeline.

Even though she hadn't played a note since the night at the restaurant, Tera's fingers still knew what to do, and the music for this album wasn't exactly what you would call challenging. She wasn't without error, but all in all it was a great performance for the project. That's what the other musicians said, anyway.

While playing, Tera looked up from the piano a few times, past the guitarists, to see Luca behind the glass in the sound booth. It looked like Luca was having a field day, excitedly asking endless questions to the sound engineers about their equipment and software. The men in the booth didn't seem to mind him being there, though. They enjoyed talking about their gear, the same as any cop would enjoy talking about theirs. While the band played, Luca seemed absolutely mystified. Laughing inside, Tera wondered if he'd ever listened to music before.

When it was over, he spent the entire drive back talking, quite energetically, mostly in Italian. He said more on that drive than she had heard him say all week. More than once she was concerned that he wouldn't make a turn because both of his hands were off the wheel. He told her about his favorite bands, and what it was like when he first heard them - why he loved them - how he felt when he listened to them. He told her about his favorite songs, his favorite CDs, his favorite singers. He just went on and on.

The sun was starting to set over the horizon, barely visible at times through the ancient buildings of the city. The sky turned a beautiful bright orange. Tera thought about how much more beautiful it would look in the country. As they approached her building, Luca started to slow down and change topics.

"And none of this would have happened today if you hadn't called me…" he said, slowing down, "Thank you. Thank you for giving me your Saturday."

"Yeah, we really made a whole day out of this, didn't we…" she started to feel a little anxious, and discreetly unfastened her seatbelt.

"I think you are a very captivating person," Luca went on to say, and Tera sat and listened politely until they pulled into the building's lot, coming to a stop, at which point she hurriedly opened the door and hopped out before the car was even in park.

"Ok, thanks so much, bye!" She closed the car door and rushed off to the building entrance. Luca, flustered, put the car in park, opened his door, and got out quickly, looking over the hood as Tera reached her door.

"*Co...sa?*" He called out to her, in some amount of shock, "Hey!"

She unlocked the door, waved, and disappeared inside the entrance - leaving him in oblivion.

Maybe she was being a coward, but running away from the police didn't seem like a bad option this time. She decided not to think about what she just did, and walked down the long hallway to the elevator. She took a left and walked down another long hall, which ended at an outside door to the common green space that was housed within the closed apartment complex. Tera felt strangely comfortable living on the ground floor, so near the enclosed outdoors.

Key in hand, she unlocked her door at the end of the hall and walked into the disheveled apartment. A few things were in the right place, but she hadn't unpacked anything yet. She set up her bed frame and maneuvered her box spring and mattress into place. She started to call Maria, but quickly ended the call. If Luca had had her phone for that long, he might have bugged it. She looked it over carefully.

She noticed the camera app was open, containing several ridiculous pictures of the two Marcos. That made her laugh. She took a small piece of dark-colored packing tape off of a box and carefully fit it over her phone camera, just in case. After looking extensively at other areas of her phone, she eventually turned the whole thing off. She couldn't remember the last time she turned off her phone. It felt isolating. Staring at the room around her, she found her African knife and started to open boxes. She opened her box of dirty dishes and sighed. She set it by her new sink, by the dishwasher. She looked at the dishwasher and smiled. "This is a game-changer," she thought.

She made good progress with her things but quit after an hour or so to go to bed. It was still fairly early, but she was very tired. Even if they didn't have any of the shooter's DNA now, it would only be a matter of time before they tested everything from last night. What would it take to get her laptop back? Maybe she could use that opportunity to get the sponge.

16

Sunday.

The next morning was a little disorienting. Tera woke up several times in the night, a few times leaping to her feet, thinking she heard a sound. Every time she fell back asleep she would have a crazy dream, all of which seemed to have the same ending: someone pulls out a gun, she runs away, and then she crashes into Luca. Then she would wake up. It was a vicious cycle.

The unfamiliar rooms in that new apartment seemed possessed by some kind of evil. Tera hoped this feeling would go away after getting her things sorted out - and some art hung up on the blank, intimidating walls. She had no clock, but when she did decide to get up, she figured by the position of the sun that she had already missed church. And lunch. She got dressed and turned on her phone. Nine missed calls, seven voicemails, four texts. She never felt so popular.

The first voicemail was from Luca. That made sense, Tera thought. The next four were from Maria. The sixth one caused Tera to pause. It was from Carlos Di Maggio, her dead boss's son. The remaining voicemail was from Maria again. She looked at her texts. They were all from Maria, wondering how yesterday went. Tera played back the voicemails:

"Buongiorno. Sovrintendente Luca Conti, della Polizia Centrale di Foggia. *Uh, hey, we have your laptop. You should... come by and get it. I'll be here until five.* Grazie, arrivederci."

"*Tera! What is going on!!!*"

"*Tera, you need to call me, tell me what happened!!!*"

"*Hey Tera, is everything going ok? I didn't see you at church this morning. A lot of people have been asking me about you, and I don't know what to tell them! Call me and tell me that you are ok, ok? And, I still really, REALLY want to know about yesterday!* Ciao.*"

"*Tera, it's Maria. I don't have your new address. Please tell me where you live so we can come over. Ok, thank you, bye-bye.*"

"Ciao Tera. Questo è Carlos, [long pause] dammi una chiamata quando puoi. Grazie."

"*Hel-LO! Tera, We are at your new apartment building, but I don't know which number you are. Please come let us in!!! I will keep calling.*"

After listening to the last message, Tera rushed over to the kitchen and grabbed her keys. She left her apartment and ran down the long halls to the front door, opened it, but didn't see anyone.

"Maria?" she called out.

"Ehi!!!" Tera heard the high pitched squeal from across the lot. Maria and her sisters had been walking between the building's various entrances for the last few minutes.

"Tera! You live so close to our cousins now. We went to your old apartment and got your address from your landlord..." They came with arms full of gifts: eggplant parmesan and homemade bread from their family, handwritten cards from various members at the church, a bottle of red wine from the pastor, and a wrapped icon of St. Peregrine from Sig.ra Bianchi. Maria chatted the whole way into the apartment, her sisters following quietly.

They made it inside - Tera quickly moved boxes and dishes off the kitchen table, so that they could set everything down.

"Oh, this is nice!" Maria said, walking around the boxes through the rooms. "A little modern..." she touched the countertops in the bathroom, and whispered loudly to her sisters,

"Nicer than the ones in our house. We should tell father." Her younger sisters looked around and nodded quietly.

"Have you eaten anything?" Tera asked.

"Have we eaten anything... Tera, you sound like mother. Yes, we lunched at home."

"I'm sorry that I missed church," Tera sat on her bed, "I had my phone off, and didn't sleep well."

"Well, you missed a good sermon," Maria said, sternly. "But everybody wanted to know where you were. They prayed for you today. You, and everyone from the shooting."

Maria and her sisters started to help Tera unpack while Maria listed off the names of everyone who came up to them at church, and what they said, and how she replied. Tera ate some of the eggplant parmesan before joining them with a box of books.

After an hour or so, the four sisters made their way to the door - they needed to go back to the church for a prayer meeting. Tera asked them to stay longer, so after a bit of discussion, Maria decided to stay behind with Tera. When they finished saying goodbye to her younger sisters, Maria picked up one of Tera's sofa pillows and started to hit Tera with it.

"Now what happened yesterday!!!" she grunted, while Tera laughed, warding off the pillow attack with a baking sheet.

"You should know," Tera said, "I know that you called while we were moving."

"Ah!!!" Maria screamed. "I can't believe it! He has a very nice voice, Tera. He speaks kindly, very formal. But he didn't tell me anything!"

"You talked for two minutes," Tera retorted, but still speaking at a reasonable volume.

"So?" Maria put the pillow back on the couch, fluffing it. "What was his name again?"

Tera looked at Maria and rolled her eyes slowly, landing her gaze on the floor.

"Luca."

"Loooooka," Maria teased her. "Yes, that is a good name. I have an uncle named Luca."

"I don't know where to begin," Tera sat down on the couch.

"Well," Maria said, "You called him, and he showed up?"

"He brought some friends... military buddies I think. You would like them, but they're Catholic. One was able to pick up that table by himself," Tera pointed to the coffee table. Maria looked intrigued.

"And, uh, afterward we all got pizza, and Luca and I talked... for quite a while... Oh, Maria!" Tera's tone suddenly became more excited.

"Last night was my gig for the *Avidità* album. It went really well! We recorded four songs, and I even improvised a solo, which was so great for me!" Tera held up her hands to her heart and fell sideways on the couch. "And for about an hour, I forgot all about the shooting. It was..." she closed her eyes, "Amazing."

Maria sat down on the floor in the middle of the room, crossing her legs. She had half a smile on her face, nodding. Maria sighed.

"How are you doing?" she asked Tera, a little timid.

"You know," Tera spoke a little fast, "Sometimes I worry that I'm pushing myself too hard, but then things like last night happen, and it is so good for my heart and my head. I'm glad I didn't cancel that gig, because it helped me so much to be there. Music has such a powerful way of mending violence. And I felt safe in that studio, which is something you take for granted... feeling safe."

Maria let out some comforting "Mmmm"s as Tera spoke, looking concerned and wanting to help.

"Was the policeman there with you?" Maria asked slowly, looking keenly at her, before cracking a large smile. Tera looked back at Maria.

"Yes... and I won't lie, it felt great knowing that there was a gun near me all day." Tera was referring to Luca as "the gun," but suddenly felt an empty feeling inside of her, as she realized she didn't know where HER gun was. She sat up and looked at Maria.

"What?" Maria looked startled. Tera stuffed a pillow into her face, screaming into it.

"So many things, Maria. So many things. The police took my computer. And I think they also took my gun. Hang on." She double-checked a few unpacked boxes before she picked up her phone and dialed Luca's number. Maria didn't know what to do, so she remained seated on the floor, watching Tera pace the room angrily as the phone rang.

"*Pronto?*"

"Hello. It's Tera. Will you please help me out? I'm missing things. Important things. And I don't know if things are missing because I lost them, or because the forensics team walked off with them, and part of me is afraid that some of my things got stolen, and it's freaking me out."

"What are you missing?"

"That's a very good question, isn't it?" She sounded really mad. "Can't you get me a list of all the things that they took? Don't I have a right to that kind of information? Isn't there some rule they have to follow, some law, to inform people of what things they take?"

There was a slight pause. "Please?" She added.

"I will see what I can do," he said. She hung up the phone.

"Who did you just call? Did you just call the police?" Maria asked, wide-eyed.

"It's so stupid!" Tera exclaimed under her breath. "They came into my apartment, Maria. Not this one, the old one. Before I moved. They came in the middle of the night, and they kicked me out, and they took my stuff."

"What? Why?" Maria asked, standing up.

"Because I accidentally woke up my neighbors," she waved her hands. "And because I was at the shooting, they decided it was significant enough to search all my things and take my stuff, just in case I was hiding something."

"That's terrible!" Maria said. "When did *this* happen?"

"Uhh… Two days ago." She picked up a hammer and some nails. Smoldering, Tera looked at Maria.

"Ok, let's put some art on the walls."

17

An hour or so later the two of them walked to the police station. It took about twenty minutes to get there, and the fresh air did Tera some good. Maria said she wanted to meet all of the policemen. "That might happen," Tera told her, thinking about her possible arrest. They walked inside the front door, and Tera marched up to the glass window. It was a bright-blonde policewoman with dark eyebrows, who Tera didn't recognize.

"*Buon pomeriggio,*" Tera said, "*Sono qui per ritirare un oggetto.*"

"*Nome, per favore?*"

"*Tera Laurito.*"

She gave the agent her papers - her passport, visa, and gun license - through the little slot in the glass. The agent left the window and walked to the back of the room. She looked at a big box on the floor, checking a slip attached. Tera put her hands into the pockets of her baggy pants, bouncing a little with impatience. The woman returned to the window and began to fill out a form, then passed it to Tera to read and sign.

"Mmm…" Tera looked it over and glanced up at the woman. "*I've had a change of address.*"

"*Ok. Have you been visited by the authorities yet?*"

"*Yes. Wait... no. Not for my change of residence.*"

"*OK then... You need to visit the local registry office at District Council. Ok?*"

The policewoman returned Tera her papers and handed her another form, which she quickly filled out. She signed the first document and returned both forms through the slot. The woman stapled the two together, put them in a stack, and walked back to the box. She picked it up and walked out of the room, out of sight.

A second later she came out the hall door to the lobby and carefully handed the box to Tera. It was a little heavy. Tera set the box on a chair, thanking the woman, who returned through the hall door.

"What's in this box?" Maria asked.

"I thought I knew... but now I don't." Tera looked at it warily before opening it. Under the interlacing cardboard flaps were a few plastic bags and two larger, thick envelopes, surrounding a bouquet of flowers that took up most of the box.

"Hmm..." Maria looked at Tera with playful eyes. "*Delfinie... e ranuncoli...*" Maria was pointing and naming various blooms within the simple assortment. Reaching past the flowers, Tera took out a medium-sized envelope. She opened it, and partially pulled out the contents, revealing her Smith & Wesson semi-automatic. She let out a long sigh of relief and peered at Maria with a smile, who was still looking at the flowers. Looking deeper into the open envelope, she noticed the loose magazine had been emptied out; she would

116

need to buy more bullets. Maria took out the bouquet. There was a handwritten note attached, which Tera snatched up immediately, but let Maria follow along. It read:

Tera,
forensics permitted me to look at a list of what was taken from you, but would not release this information for distribution. Anyway, I was able to retrieve a few additional pieces for you.
Yours,
Luca

"Wow… he was very quick about this, wasn't he? And do you see that?" Maria whispered in Tera's ear, "He says that he is yours." They exchanged a glance, Tera suppressing an embarrassed laugh, then turned back to the box. The larger envelope contained Tera's laptop. The bags contained Tera's toothbrush, toothpaste, a pair of scissors, and a lighter. Tera picked up the bag with the scissors in it.

"I wondered where these were…" she said quietly. It bothered her to know that the Carabinieri had searched her apartment well enough to find things that she couldn't find herself.

"That's it?" Maria asked.

"For now…" Tera's mind tried to decipher what all this meant. These things were being returned to her because the forensics team no longer needed them. That would seem to imply that they hadn't yet tested the sponge. Or, more likely, they were done testing everything, but Luca didn't think Tera would want the sponge. She was probably too late. It would be a manner of hours before they showed up to arrest her, and bring her back for more questioning.

"Are you ok?" Maria asked, concerned. "You don't look well…" Tera looked at Maria and said nothing. She felt hopeless. She might as well confess everything now and hope for the best. But, no, she couldn't do that. If they knew the shooter was at her apartment, they would want to know why he was there - why she lied about it.

"If you truly value your life…" The shooter's words rang through her mind "you'll keep this little meeting a secret." If she told the police the truth, and they believed her, they would want her to identify the man. If she did, mysterious men would pop out of the cracks of Italy and ruin her life. If she refused to identify the man, she would become a prime suspect. And a big target. If there was any way for her to get into the lab without being noticed, to get to that sponge, that would be her best strategy. Until then, she needed to keep quiet.

Maria sat down next to Tera and gave her a hug, not knowing what else to do.

"It's going to be ok. You're not alone," she said. Tera remembered people saying that to her years ago, after the funerals. Speaking of funerals, tomorrow was the memorial service for the local victims of the shooting. Thinking about this reminded Tera that she needed to call Carlos back. They should get going. Tera returned the hug and stood up. She went back to the window.

"*Mi scusi, c'è Sovrintendente Conti?*"

"*No, lui non è qui adesso.*" The blonde woman replied. Tera looked at Maria,

"I don't understand, he said he would be here until five." Tera looked back to the woman behind the window.

"*Sai dove si trova?*" she asked.

"*Il sovrintendente ha dovuto rispondere a un'emergenza.*"

"Oh. We must have just missed him," Tera said. "Well," looking at Maria, "I guess we'll have to come back another time."

They took turns carrying the box on the way back to the apartment. They took a roundabout route back because Tera wanted to look at the *Fontana del Sele* - an enormous, beautiful fountain installed in the middle of the *Piazza Cavour*, which was basically a large traffic circle. Tera thought about all the things she would miss if she had to leave, or be locked up. This was one of her favorite places in the city when it wasn't crowded.

The old fountain was situated near the *Pronao Della Villa*, a neoclassical aqueduct. This nearby structure was a beautiful stretch of stone, supported by twenty-eight white-marble columns in two rows. On the other side was a much smaller fountain, and a spotting of palms and other flora, dissipating into the park. Tera had heard that every now and then a winter will find Foggia just cold enough to dust these palms with snow.

As the fountain came into her sights, Tera handed Maria the box and emptied her pockets into it. She looked down at her Chaco sandals and briefly examined her right foot. Then, without a word of explanation, she ran toward the water basin and, dodging a car, hopped over the edge and climbed in. This was the kind of disrespectful thing that idiotic tourists did, and that Tera had always secretly wanted to do. She figured she had nothing to lose now.

She made her way towards the middle and climbed the decorative rocks in the center to hug the protruding structure that distributed the water, now towering over her. She made a wish and sat in the chilly pool with her eyes closed, under a falling stream of water. It washed over her short hair and bare shoulders like a cold shower. It didn't take long for a security guard to run over, yelling at her,

"Esci! Esci!"

She wriggled her way over the edge and started running.

Maria just stood there in shock, holding the box, watching the security guard chase Tera, soaking wet, several blocks down the dusty sidewalks. Eventually the security guard stopped, frustrated, and started making his way back. Maria tried to look casual as she slowly made her way across the street to follow Tera's path.

She found her before too long - still dripping, with a big smile on her face - sitting under a young tree on the sidewalk, holding her foot.

"Feel better?" Maria asked, confused and disappointed. Tera kept smiling.

"Yeah, yeah, I think so. It felt good to run…" she laughed, "and not get caught."

Tera stood up and shook her hair out like a dog. Maria reached out and picked at Tera's wet locks.

"Well, now you are going to get sick, if we do not hurry and dry your hairs!"

"What? No, I'm fine. Relax."

"You are a crazy foreigner…" Maria sighed.

They walked together for a while before talking again. It was a sunny day, but still cool in temperature, so Tera stayed out of the shade as much as she could to stay warm.

"I can't imagine what this is like for you…" Maria said quietly, and not without emotion. Tera kept her hands in her baggy wet pockets.

"It's a bit scary," Tera said. "I don't know what's going on with me half the time either." Tera's hair was almost completely dry now, her tank-top still changing to a lighter color as the water slowly departed from it.

"Sometimes," Tera said, "I feel like everything is closing in on me, and I just want to curl up and hide. It's such a horrible feeling, to be so afraid. So powerless. To want to have control over the situation, over myself, and to not be able to do even that." They rounded a corner to a charming, colorful side street.

"Other times," Tera continued, "I feel so mad, just so, so mad." Maria looked at Tera.

"Here," Maria handed Tera the box, "Use some of your anger to carry this for a while."

"Thanks," Tera smiled. "It's like, being angry is the only thing I can do to stop being so afraid. But I don't know how to connect with anyone while I'm being so angry. I just get so self-focussed and selfish. So closed off."

Maria looked up at the sky for a minute. "You feel closed in, so you close yourself off?" She looked at Tera. "At least you are able to talk about it so openly!" she said. "I believe this is the first good step to take."

"Yeah?" Tera felt encouraged. "Walking really is good therapy..."

They made it back to the apartment a little before five. Tera took a shower while Maria helped organize sheet music. They ate a quick meal together and talked more about the past. About men. About how being single was a blessing. They talked about jazz music, and about police uniforms.

Tera walked Maria to the nearby bus stop and saw her off. Tera would see her tomorrow at the memorial service, if she wasn't arrested by then. Tera sat on her couch, feeling much better about how the apartment looked. But it was like sitting in someone else's home. She called Carlos.

"*Hmm... pronto,*" he answered.

"*Hi, it's Tera Laurito. I'm calling you back.*"

18

Tera always thought of Carlos as kind of a punk kid. He spoke informally, had tattoos, a nose ring, and usually wore these brightly colored feather earrings that hung down to his shoulders. But tonight he looked different. His piercings were more subtle, and he looked more grown-up. They met in a small *osteria*, half a kilometer from Tera's apartment. She made it inside before the sun went down.

"Thanks for meeting me," Carlos said, feebly. He poked at his dark, moppy hair. *"Have you talked to any of the others?"*

"From The Golden Flower? No," Tera took her jacket off and laid it over the back of her seat.

"Stefania is still in the hospital." He scratched the top of his long nose. *"She had a bad reaction to the drug. She is in a coma."*

"What drug?" Tera asked.

"The drug from the shooting. Stefania suffers from sleep apnea, so they think that's why she is responding this way. Asia and Cristian have been staying with her family, night and day, to help with the children."

"I didn't know there was a drug." Tera felt awful for Stefania. While they weren't close, Tera always thought she had a great personality. She often worked behind the bar with Carlos.

"Mmhmm." Carlos tapped his hands together at the fingertips. *Three people were attacked with drugs. Stefania, Davide, and my mother. Forensics reported that it was Midazolam.*

"Mida-what?" Tera asked.

"Eh... Midazolam... o... Versed." Carlos stared into Tera's eyes. *"It's a common sedative... anticonvulsant."* Carlos reached over and tapped behind his left shoulder, *"There was a needle in their back, ten milligrams. Knocked them unconscious."*

Carlos mumbled a few other things, just quickly enough that Tera didn't understand what he was saying. He stopped a nearby server and, looking grim, ordered a complicated drink. He and the server talked about it for a while before Carlos ended up writing down exactly what he wanted on a napkin. Tera ordered champagne. Already confused, the server asked what the occasion was.

"Being alive?" Tera said, unintentionally sounding adorable to Carlos. The server smiled and darted off.

"How have you been?" Carlos asked, rather curious.

"Uh," Tera started, *"Not great. Not great."* Carlos nodded quickly for a moment.

"I heard that you spoke to the man. To the shooter." He looked disgusted.

"Yeah..." Tera was deep in thought, remembering that only moments before she exchanged words with that man, several people lost their lives in a flash, by his hand.

"He... didn't kill me for some reason." She looked over to the playbills posted on the wall across from their table. *"I don't know why,"* she said, sincerely baffled. Carlos muttered a few

short sounds that Tera couldn't discern. There was a man on the other side of the room playing his electric guitar into a crummy sound system, creating an unsettling mood that added to the already emotionally unstable environment.

"How is your mom doing? You said she was hurt?" Carlos nodded quickly, staring through the table.

"She is better, she is better." He rubbed his mouth with his hand. *"Magari..."* he murmured. *"Without Papà, I don't know what will happen next."* He ran his hand down his face slowly, then wiped his nose with a partial fist. *"I don't know what to do."* Tears began to emerge from both eyes, though he fought them back. The server came back with their drinks, set them on the table. Carlos waved the server away while hiding his face. He pushed his drink aside and continued to fidget with his hands. Tera looked at her sparkling champagne. This might be her last drink before Italian Prison. She took a long, slow sip, trying to enjoy it amidst the bitter atmosphere.

"When were the people hurt with the drug? I never heard about this." Tera asked this when Carlos had better composed himself.

"Mah..." Carlos waved his hand, *"minutes before the shooting began, they think. They tested mamma at the lab for several hours, trying to figure out exactly what was in her system."*

Tera perked up.

"The lab?" she asked.

"Yeah, where they took the bodies."

"Oh." She paused. *"The morgue?"*

"No... not dead bodies. The living, unconscious bodies."

Tera looked at him with squinty eyes, not understanding.

"The hospital?"

"No... Laboratorio forense." He spoke a little slower, if not a tad condescendingly. *"After the police arrived at The Golden Flower they took the three people who were unconscious to the lab where they test things for science and medicine. Do you understand?"*

Tera nodded; Carlos looked a bit confused, as she seemed happy to hear this.

"Why?" Tera asked, *"Why not the hospital?"*

"I think it is the same building. But I am not really sure."

Carlos looked over at his drink. He blinked hard a few times, then reached for it and took a sip.

"Who did it? Who drugged them?" Tera tried to calm herself down, and not seem too interested.

"It had to be the shooter," he said. Tera looked at her phone. It was almost eight o'clock.

"Wow," she said, now very distracted. *"I'm sorry to hear that. Is there anything else you wanted to talk about?"* She took another slow sip of champagne, which was tricky because now her hand was beginning to tremble. But it tasted sweeter this time.

"Sì," Carlos nodded. *"I'm going to sell the restaurant. I thought you should all know, you know, before tomorrow's memorial service. There will be an announcement to the media. Oh, and..."* he reached into his leather bag, and wiped his nose again, *"I wanted to settle your accounts. You never got paid for Monday."* He pulled out a checkbook, pen, and ledger. He went over the numbers with her, very much like how his father would have done, and wrote her a check. He put his things away, and Tera finished her champagne. Carlos had hardly touched his drink. Tera flagged down a server, to give them her card, but Carlos put his hand on hers,

"*Permettimi*," he handed the server a couple of paper euros. *"There's one more thing, Tera,"* Carlos said, trying to keep her from running out on him.

"*Sì?*" She relaxed her shoulders and sank back into her chair. Carlos paused for a while.

"Despite what you may think - despite what people say... I know that my Papà was not a good man. He was deeply troubled. He told many lies, and had many secrets. And while I wish he was still here, I do not think it was a crime that he was also killed that night." He looked up at Tera.

"What kind of person am I, to say that about my own Papà?" He took a long hard drink. *"I believe he was protecting Garbazzi. Maybe even helping him. I don't know how involved he was, but I believe he was the reason... that everyone died that night. The reason the shooter was there."* He looked at Tera. *"I'm sorry. I'm sorry that you had to... see everything that you saw."*

Tera didn't know how to feel, but she knew that if she were in Carlos's position, it would be easy to be burdened by this forever. She reached out and took his hands in hers.

"Don't apologize for your father, Carlos. If you do, you will spend your whole life apologizing for the mistakes of others. And don't ever blame yourself. You can only move forward." He squeezed her hands and nodded. They sat for another minute without speaking,

listening to the sounds of clinking glasses and muted conversations, all wrapped up in the sad music of their hearts.

After leaving, Tera made a few quick errands, then took a stroll in the evening air, now cooling off. She made her way past those small mobs that crowded the alleys outside of clubs. She watched headlights dance on the stone walls of ancient buildings, in and out of the meandering streets. She eventually stopped in a little cafe that was still open, sat in a chair by the window, and sent a text.

Hey Luca, If ur not busy, could you meet me @ Cafè di Mezzanotte? I'll be here till 23:30. Thanks. -Tera

She stared at the old newspaper articles that were decoupaged onto the small round table in front of her. She didn't want to manipulate Luca. But she was willing to. She didn't know how much time she had left, if any. Maybe he already knew. She wondered whether or not he was romantically interested in her, and if that would change anything. She blinked at the wall.

She normally ignored men who asked her out and tried to buy her things. They were usually annoying and over-the-top. But Luca wasn't like that. He was kind, and seemed to genuinely care about her. So what if everything - the looks, the readiness to help, the flowers - what if Luca was only being kind? Only being Italian? Maybe he felt sorry for her. Tera had to acknowledge that Luca might be nothing more than a nice guy. A good cop. A friend. She wished she had more time to think about this, but within a few minutes she could see him outside.

19

Luca ambled through the cafe door, and seeing Tera smiling at him, skipped over to her table before landing in his seat.

"Hi!" she said, already feeling guilty inside.

"Good evening," he nodded, unzipping his leather coat. Underneath, he was still in uniform. But no hat.

"Did you just come from work?" Tera asked, a bit puzzled.

"Sort of." He looked empty. "Something came up. I needed to be there." He looked around the sparsely occupied cafe, then back at Tera.

"I saw at headquarters that you got your... toothbrush back. You must have missed that."

"So, I wanted to apologize..." Tera said, avoiding eye contact. "I wasn't very kind to you on the phone earlier. I'm sorry."

"That's ok. You were clearly upset. I wanted to resolve that quickly."

Tera looked up at Luca,

"Thank you for the flowers." She quickly turned her gaze away from his face. He nodded at her for a bit.

"I would probably be as upset," he said playfully, "If I couldn't find my - toothbrush."

He reached with his hand to his side, took his gun out from his holster, and removed the magazine. He quickly double-checked the barrel before sliding his Beretta 92FS towards Tera. She looked at the gun for an instant, then looked at Luca's face in bewilderment. Was he trying to show off, or was he just being stupid? He looked at her blankly, then gestured with his hand in an upward motion, as if to say, "go ahead." She picked up the Italian pistol and carefully handled it.

Amongst other things, Italians know how to make incredibly attractive food, cars, and guns. She slowly felt her way around the beautifully crafted tool of death.

"*Bellino...*" she said quietly.

"You like guns."

"Yeah..." She wanted to say, and do, many things that she did not. Instead, she slowly slid the gun back across the table. She couldn't understand why he would trust her like that.

"You look sad..." Luca took back the weapon. Tera nonchalantly looked down at the floor.

"Toothbrushes don't kill people..." she slowly raised her gaze to Luca. "People kill people."

Tera watched as he reloaded his gun. The magazine's click and the percussive *ker-clack* of the slide made her feel simultaneously nervous and excited. He fit his gun back onto his belt.

"The memorial service is tomorrow," he said. "Will you be there?"

Tera thought for a minute.

"I... don't know."

"I think you need to go," he said, gently. "The others would be encouraged to see you there. You can all help each other - process the event, together."

Tera said nothing.

"I could pick you up."

Tera looked at him, suddenly attentive. Her eyes darted back and forth in thought.

"Yeah, that's a good idea, actually." She looked worried, and Luca was squinting at her, trying to read her.

"Which car are you driving tomorrow?"

"Do you have a preference?" he asked, under a laugh.

"Black seems more appropriate. But aren't you working tomorrow?"

"No..." Luca said, deeply concerned with the thoughts in his head.

Tera took a deep breath.

"Ten o'clock?" She looked a little restless.

"Ten? The service is at four."

"There's a meeting, in the morning, for the family and survivors."

Luca nodded and smiled.

"I could come earlier if you like. Nine?" he suggested.

"No. Ten is better," she said firmly. She gradually reached her hand into her pocket and took out her keys. She put them on the table and looked at them fearfully. Luca kept his eyes on Tera.

"So…" she said, while sliding off a ring with two keys on it. "This probably seems weird, but…" she handed the keys across the table to Luca. "I'd really like you to have these." He took them and looked at her with curious enthrallment.

"These are…?"

"A key to my mailbox," Tera pointed to the smaller of the two keys, and put the rest of her keys back into her pocket, looking more resolved. "I think I'm going to *Napoli* next week, to look for work. I will be gone for a while, and I was hoping you could pick up my mail for me while I'm gone?"

"Oh," Luca seemed mildly disappointed to hear that, but then a bit serious. "Yes, I can do that for you."

"And that's a spare key to my new apartment."

Luca blinked at her, holding the keys. She looked from side to side. Luca looked at the larger key and then blinked some more. His face reacted with strange understanding and confusion.

"Really?"

"Don't think about it too much," Tera put her hands on the table, then, looking a little skittish, "I just, I think you should have one, because…" she stared intently at the wall next to them, tapping all of her fingers on the table, as many pianists tend to do. "I would feel safer knowing you had a key." Then, looking at Luca, "And the last time the police came to my apartment, they busted the door."

Tera stood up abruptly and pushed in her chair. Luca sat, holding the keys, watching Tera walk towards the exit as she tied up her jacket. He flew out of his seat and caught up to her, just outside the door.

"Do you need a ride home?"

"I'd prefer to walk, thanks."

"Ok," he said, zipping up his coat, following along with her. She shouldn't have been surprised that he was walking her home. It wasn't far, and it was getting late; Tera knew it was better to not be alone.

"I'm sorry that I wasn't in today when you stopped by," he said. The air was crisp and cool. The sky was cloudy, and it felt like it might rain. He went on,

"I was able to get more information about that phone number."

"Oh yeah?" Tera picked up her head.

"I called a unit in *Roma*. They found the source of the call."

Tera's heart began to beat faster, and she felt suddenly afraid. This might have been a big mistake.

"It was a cell phone. They found the signal was, well... it was coming from a cell phone in Foggia."

"What does that mean?" she asked, counting the remaining blocks home.

"Someone smart, with access to some sophisticated equipment, gave you that call. And they didn't want to be found. But, we traced the location of the phone itself. It was in a trashcan, near the hospital, not too far from here." Tera didn't know what to say or think about this.

"We couldn't find anything on where the phone came from. Unfortunately, this makes the mystery just interesting enough that now the Carabinieri have decided to look into it too." Luca looked at Tera.

"I'm afraid it makes you look very suspicious to them."

"That's not fair," Tera grumbled. "What did I do?"

"I told them that you volunteered this information. I think that makes you look good. It helps a lot when we hear it from you first."

"Really?" Tera said. "Ok. Today I committed a civil infraction."

Luca laughed.

"Oh yes? What horrible thing did you do?"

"No, I'm serious," she said, a little too proud. "I intentionally broke the law, and then I got away with it. It was really exhilarating." She now had a big smile on her face, which Luca couldn't stop wondering at.

"You're not going to tell me what it was?" he asked, a little miffed.

"It's more fun if you try to guess," she said cheerfully.

Tera was amazed at the things that he guessed. Police officers see it all, she thought. They got to the apartment building, Luca still rattling off petty crimes.

"You insulted a judge?"

"No."

"You… assaulted a judge?"

"No."

"Did you set something on fire?"

"No."

They reached the door, and Tera went digging for her keys.

"Allow me," Luca unlocked the door with his newly acquired gift. Tera's heart skipped a beat. He opened the door and ushered her into the long hallway, following her inside.

"Did you spit on a judge?"

"No. How is that different from insulting a judge?"

"Oh, good point. Actually, spitting would be considered an assault. Did you drive a car today?"

"No."

"Hmm… that removes several other possibilities. Did you damage someone's property?"

"No."

They reached the elevators and turned left. Tera wasn't sure what to expect when they reached her door. She started walking a little slower.

"Ok… did you try to leave the country?"

"No."

"Did you leave the city?"

"No."

"Did you steal something?"

Tera paused and stopped in the hall. She looked carefully at the floor.

"No." She kept walking.

"You had to think about that!" Luca was greatly amused. "How interesting. Do you own a goldfish?"

"What? No…"

"Did you tell a lie to a judge?"

"*Mamma mia*, will you stop asking me about judges? I had absolutely zero interaction with judges today, ok?"

"Well then, you really have me, Tera. I thought for sure that was your crime. The only other things I can think of are that you either took a bath in a public fountain, or you made love in an automobile. And I have a hard time imagining you doing either of those things."

They reached her door.

"That's good to know," she said, unlocking the door with her key. She was going to say, "thank you for walking me home," but she wasn't quick enough. His lips were on hers in a moment, his right hand softly holding her head, while his left arm embraced her. It happened so naturally, so easily. Tera felt comfortable in his arms, and the warmth of this contact caught Tera more off guard than the kiss itself. His face slowly pulled away from hers, and she felt herself slip back through her door, leaving him in the hall.

"I lied. I spat on a judge." She closed the door in front of her, locking it. She knew that wasn't worth much. She had given him a key. A mad rush of emotions overcame her, she felt all at once exuberant, embarrassed, guilty, angry, and suddenly incredibly lonely. It was more than she could push back, stuff down, or put out of her mind. She tried to fight it, but soon began sobbing uncontrollably, leaning her back against the door. She slowly slid down to the ground in a curled up ball, gasping for air: a heartbroken doorstop. It didn't matter what she tried to do, her emotions were stronger than her mind could reason, and there was nothing for her to do now except sit on the floor and cry. She put her hands over her mouth, in an attempt to keep herself quiet.

After a few minutes, she heard Luca's voice through the door. He had to have been sitting on the other side, because his voice was so close to her ears. He was speaking so gently.

"Little bird, please do not cry. It makes my heart ache to know that you are sad. Please, do not be dismayed. If you would allow me, I would hold you in my arms in an instant. Oh Tera, I hardly know you, and yet my heart is so full of care for you. Please, do not be sad."

Tera couldn't speak, but his words helped her to breathe. She leaned her head back against the door, tears flowing from her closed eyes.

"May I tell you a story?" He continued. *"When I was thirteen years old, my father was shot and killed. He was a policeman, working a job. I remember the day that Alfredo came to tell my mother that my father was dead. After the funeral, I told my mother that I would never be a policeman, so that she would not have to worry about losing me the way she lost her husband. And do you know what my mother said to me? She told me that she loved my father, and that she was proud to know that he died while helping others. She said she was not afraid of my father dying, because her love was stronger than her*

fear. Do you know this, Tera? In love there is no fear. They say that perfect love chases fear away."

Tera opened her eyes. She continued to breathe as she could. The tears, still coming, were becoming less painful. She didn't feel alone anymore.

20

Luca sat with his back to Tera's door for a few seconds more before he heard a neighbor coming down the hall. He was still in uniform, which meant that like it or not, he was still on duty. He stood up, so as not to draw attention, but it didn't make much of a difference. The man turned the corner, and recognizing the striped pants on the policeman in the hallway, was a bit startled.

"Is something wrong?" the man asked.

"*Buona sera, Signore,*" Luca said, loud enough to ensure Tera could hear him through the door. *"Everything is alright. How are you this evening?"*

"Oh…" the man reacted, a bit relieved, but also a bit wary. *"Are you here to take care of that car?"* Luca raised an eyebrow.

"What car are you referring to?"

"Oh…" the man pointed back down the long hall to the parking lot. *"There is a car, it has been in an unauthorized parking spot for two months. It prevents those of us who live here from being able to park there. It needs to be towed."*

Luca really didn't want to deal with this right now. He'd had a very long and very trying day, and all he could think about was Tera. He inwardly cursed his ardent sense of duty before walking with the man towards the parking lot.

"Did you address this with your landlord?" Luca asked.

"Oh... yes, but he does nothing!" the man said to him, going on and on about the agreement that all the tenants have to sign about the parking policy, and how these rules are rarely enforced. It was beginning to mist outside, and Luca immediately regretted not having his cap. The man showed Luca the car, parked crooked across two spaces. Luca got out his notepad and wrote down the plate number, along with some additional information from the exasperated fellow.

As soon as he was able to break free, Luca bid the man a good night and headed away down the sidewalk. The walk was bitter for Luca. He wanted nothing more than to help Tera, but he knew how it would look to have a cop looming around her apartment after midnight. The street lights created an orange atmosphere in the now heavy mist that was filling the air. He could feel the cold air press against his face as he walked quickly down the few blocks.

He was pleased with the results of the bouquet. Earlier that day he had fumbled around the flower shop long enough for the florist to ask him what the occasion was. Luca told him it was for an apology. The florist glared at him before asking *"What did you do?"* Luca shrugged and told him, *"I am not sure."* The florist asked him *"Do you love this woman?"* and Luca again said *"I am not sure,"* at which point the florist's mother burst into the conversation and told Luca to shut up. She informed him that she had the perfect bouquet for *"the man who doesn't know."* And he had to hand it to her. Those beautiful blooms seemed to effectively cover over whatever it was he had done to offend Tera. She must have truly appreciated the gesture, to go from running away from him - to giving him her key.

Luca couldn't help but smile as he thought about their kiss. Tera tasted a bit like champagne. He thought several times about turning around. He finally reached his blue Alfa Romeo, climbed in, and put his cap back on. He thought about how differently this night could have gone if he'd only had a change of clothes with him in the police car - Tera's key was burning a hole through his pocket. He dreaded going home, but knew that sooner or later he would have to.

He drove straight back to his place. He hung his hat and coat on a rack. Threw his keys onto a side table: a minor crash that echoed through his one-bedroom apartment. He took off his utility belt and his police shirt, watching in the bathroom mirror as he slowly transformed from *Sovrintendente* Conti into ordinary Luca Conti. He washed his face and brushed his teeth. He took a moment to look at his toothbrush.

Luca locked his gun in a safe. He poured a tall glass of water and slowly drank it down. He plugged in his cell phone to the charger near the bed, before climbing in. He moved carefully, trying not to wake up his sleeping wife. He closed his eyes and thought about his father. He thought about what kind of a man he was becoming himself.

21

Monday.

The morning came soon enough for Luca. He was awake at six and out the door by seven. He drove his squad car back to the station, to exchange it for the Audi. He loaded a packed bag into the little trunk of the black car. He stood outside the two vehicles for a minute before deciding to fill out some paperwork in his office. He had to fill the time somehow. The station was quiet, only a few police agents milling about from the late shift. He blew past the front desk at the east entrance, nodding quickly at the receptionist and security guards. He wound his way quickly through the halls and finally settled in his office. After some time, there was a knock on his door.

"*Sovrintendente?*" It was *Assistente* Bruno. She knocked again.

"*Avanti,*" he said loudly. The blonde policewoman opened the door and stood in the office entryway. Luca was sitting behind his desk, out of uniform, busily organizing forms that were scattered all over. Still holding the doorknob, she put her other hand on her hip.

"*Isn't this your day off?*" She looked a little perturbed. Luca motioned to all the paperwork on his desk. She continued, "*You were working late last night. And now you are here?*"

Assistente Bruno walked over to his desk and set down another piece of paper onto the pile. It was a timesheet of his hours from last week. *"You're working too much, sir."*

Another policeman walked past the open door and looked in.

"Sovrintendente?" It was *Agente* Ferraro. *"Have you been here all night?"*

"Buongiorno," Luca said. "No." He looked at the two of them and leaned back in his chair.

"This is what happens when you don't have a Vice Sergeant." He looked at the papers again, then pointed at *Assistente* Bruno. *"You should consider inquiring about that position during your review next month. You would probably be very good at this."*

The young woman looked proud. Ferraro looked pensive.

"Sergeant, since you are here, would you mind if I took a minute of your time?" he asked. Bruno gave a slight nod and took her leave. Ferraro entered and closed the door. He sat on the couch.

"Sir, I have concerns about the Golden Flower case. I've been thinking about this, and it doesn't make sense."

Luca leaned forward and rested his hands on the desk. Ferraro took off his cap and brushed his hair with his hand, carefully avoiding the bruises on his neck.

"The more information we gather, the less we are informed. The Carabinieri continuously take our evidence without even so much of an explanation. This kind of broken cooperation is so unusual. I cannot understand it."

"*International affairs,*"Luca explained, "*often involve many pieces left unexplained. I know it can be very frustrating, but we are never guaranteed answers. Even so, we need to do our job. We must aid the investigation in whatever way we can. Think of this as an opportunity to display your finest characteristics with your work. Cases like these offer unique challenges and often allow for the most growth.*"

Ferraro nodded and bounced his police cap on his lap.

"*Signore,*" he said, "*I have been receiving threats since Wednesday.*"

Luca responded with a curious look. "*Lettere misteriose nella mia posta,*" Ferraro pulled a few envelopes out of his inside coat pocket, threw them onto the desk. "*They all say roughly the same thing. To stop working on the Golden Flower case, or they will come for my children.*"

Luca picked up the letters and looked at Ferraro with concern.

"*Why haven't you mentioned this before?*"

"*I don't know...*"Ferraro looked at his cap. "*I suppose I was afraid.*"

Luca put his face in his hands and rubbed his forehead, letting out a groan.

"*It's just another thing...*"Luca ran his hand through his light brown hair. "*Ok, you need to call the Technical Director. Tell him everything you can about these letters. And I am sure that the Chief Inspector will want to see them as well.*"Luca looked at his watch.

"*I will call Cociarelli and the Chief Marshall.*"

Ferraro stood up and thanked the Sergeant, taking back the letters. He opened the office door.

"*Agente Ferraro,*" Luca said, "*Stai attento.*"

The man nodded and walked out.

Luca took out his phone and dialed the contact he had listed for "My Boss."

"*Ready...*"

"*Good morning sir, I'm sorry to bother you, but agent Ferraro just informed me that he is receiving threats against his life. Against his family.*"

"*Where are you right now?*" The Sgt. Chief replied.

"*I'm in my office, Sir.*"

"*Luca...*"

"*Sir?*"

"*Why are you at work so early? On your day off?*"

"*Well, I...*"

"*Go home.*"

"*Sir?*" Luca asked, timidly.

"*I will be there in twenty minutes. Thank you for following protocol, now get some damn rest.*" Alfredo hung up.

Luca looked at his phone in mild disbelief before calling Russo, whom he had listed as "The Boss." But to his confusion, the call was transferred to *Tenente* Napolitano instead.

"*Tell me,*" he answered.

"*Good morning sir, this is Sergeant Luca Conti of the Foggia Central Police. I was just informed that one of our agents has been receiving death threats by mail since Wednesday. The threats warn him to stop investigating the Golden Flower case."*

"Has the Technical Director been notified?

"That is currently underway, sir."

"Do your agents typically receive threats?"

"Not of this kind, no."

"Anything else?"

"No sir."

Napolitano hung up. Luca again looked at his phone incredulously.

"Doesn't anyone say goodbye anymore?" he murmured to himself. He looked at the remaining paperwork on his desk, then glanced at his watch. He would draft a report on this later. He got out of his chair and left the office. Walking down the hall towards the lobby, he thought about the last few days and the myriad of events that took place. *Assistente* Bruno wished him a good day as he walked out the front door to his car.

He stopped by a bakery on his way to Tera's apartment, picking up a few pastries to go. He hoped, as usual, to cheer her up. He pulled into a parking spot near her building entrance and gave her a call. What should he say when he saw her? Should he mention last night? Would it be easier not to talk about it? The phone went to Tera's voicemail and he hung up without leaving a message. He grabbed the bag of pastries, got out of his car, and walked up to the door. He let himself in.

Walking down that first long hallway he approached two women leaving the apartment, one who was carrying a baby boy. He greeted them and waved at the baby as he passed them by, eliciting some joyful squeals from the child, which brought smiles to everyone's faces. He turned the corner at the elevators, heading down the second hall. He knocked on Tera's door and waited. There was no response. Luca knocked again. There was still no response. He tried calling her one more time before getting out the key. He turned it over in his hand a couple of times before finally opening the door, calling inside.

"Hello? Tera?"

Immediately he felt the apartment was much colder than out in the hall. He stepped inside, the door closing behind him. Looking in the kitchen, he saw his bouquet of flowers sticking out of a boot in the middle of her dining room table. He admired how well put together the apartment had become since he had helped her move, only two days ago. Simultaneously, he felt a strong sense of unease. He set down the bag of pastries on the table and took out his gun. The lights were all off, with only natural light pouring in through the windows. He could hear sounds from outside. He turned to the living room to see the piano bench moved against the far wall, below an open upper window. Some rainwater had come in; the top of the bench and the floor around it were wet.

"Tera?"

He felt his heart rate increase, and quickly entered the bedroom. Her bed was unmade, her jacket on the floor, but she was not to be found. He turned around and headed back towards the entrance. As he passed the bathroom in the hall, he noticed the door was shut. He tried to open it, but it was locked. He fit his gun into his belt and jiggled the door handle to no effect. He swore under his breath before throwing his weight into the door, forcing it open.

His heart stopped. Tera was curled up on the floor near the bathtub, still wearing her clothing from yesterday. A bit of her short hair covered her face. Luca rushed to her, kneeling on the cold tile floor beside her, feeling her wrists for a pulse. Her hands were cold, but she was still alive. He moved the hair away from her eyes and caressed the side of her face, processing what to do next. He tried to wake her up gently, but she was unresponsive. He checked her airways and put his head to her chest to hear her breathing. She showed no obvious signs of injury, so he carefully moved her body and turned her onto her side. After looking at her for a few seconds he got out his cell phone and called 118.

22

Within minutes they had moved her onto a stretcher in the living room. Luca stayed as close to her as they would allow. One of the nurses, dressed in neon yellow, pointed out a tiny red dot on the back of Tera's right shoulder. The other responder looked at Luca, and the two of them immediately began to search through the apartment. This was all too familiar. They found an empty syringe in the living room trash can, under a significant amount of used tissues. Some more calls were made, and an hour later Luca once again found himself in Napolitano's face, this time inside a cramped office at the forensics lab.

"You were the one who found her?"

"Is she alright?" Luca refused to sit in the chair provided. He stood with his hands on his waist, staring down the two Carabinieri.

"Answer my questions, Sergeant, and I will let you see her."

"Yes," Luca replied. *"I found her on the floor in the apartment bathroom."*

"How did you get into her apartment?"

"She gave me a key."

Tenente Napolitano pondered this for a brief moment before raising his eyebrows at the other young man in uniform.

"I understand." He scratched his nose and looked at Luca. *"When did you arrive at the apartment?"* he asked, acting snooty.

"Ten o'clock this morning."

"Why were you there this morning?"

"She asked me to give her a ride to the meeting before the memorial service."

A forensics assistant came knocking at the door. Napolitano motioned to Luca to stay, as he stepped out. This office was not designed for interrogations. The whole building was fairly new construction and this office had two walls of floor to ceiling windows. Luca could clearly hear and see the assistant tell the Lieutenant that Tera was awake. Luca went to open the door, the other man ineffectively trying to stop him. Napolitano looked at Luca with a sneer,

"We're not done with you yet."

"I have every right to be present when you question her," Luca demanded.

"Oh, I think not Sergeant Conti. You've made it clear that you are too personally involved. Having you present would only detract from her testimony."

"You cannot question her without a member of the Foggia State Police in the..."

"You are not the only qualified member of the State Police Force. I will not have you speaking to me in this manner. You will remain in this room until further notice." Napolitano stomped his foot while pointing to the office. The other man stood nearby, looking at Luca, ready to try again.

"*Sir,*"Luca said, full of disdain, before walking back into the office. After half an hour Luca could see Leading Constable Bruno and Sgt. Chief Cociarelli in the other room, heading up the stairs to the labs. Luca, still standing, looked at the other man in the office.

"*Do you enjoy working under Lieutenant Napolitano?*" he asked in a displeased tone.

"*You are not in a position to be asking the questions,*"the man said, nervously.

"*What a prick...*"Luca said, just loudly enough to make the man flustered.

"*What are we doing here, hm?*"Luca addressed the Carabiniere. "*Are you going to ask me questions, or are we going to stand here and stare at each other?*"

"*I am following orders,*"the man said. He must not have known what else to say. It was another twenty minutes or so before Napolitano returned, walking a bit slower. He closed the door and leaned against the windows, looking at Luca. He said nothing for a full minute.

"*Sergeant Conti,*"he began slowly, in a more serious tone, "*do you have any reason to suspect that Ms. Laurito may have wished to hurt herself?*"

Luca stared back, his face gradually changing from a demeanor of anger to one of concern.

"*You think she did this to herself?*"

"*Please just answer the question.*"

"*Why would the window have been open?*"

Napolitano was bothered, but understood that Luca needed some information in order to cooperate.

"Security footage from last night showed no one enter or leave the apartment through that window. It was opened from the inside shortly after four in the morning."

Luca looked down at the ground.

"I don't understand."

"When did you last see Ms. Laurito, before this morning?"

"Late last night."

"Did she seem upset?"

Luca paused before admitting, *"Yes."*

"Hmm." The Lieutenant waved his arm at the other man and opened the door.

"Thank you. You may go."

Luca left the two of them in the office and headed slowly into the hall - not fifteen seconds later he heard their laughter behind him. He swallowed his pride and continued up the stairs to the floor with the labs. He was ushered through the locked door by an assistant, and soon joined Alfredo in the hall.

Luca leaned against the hallway wall across from the Sgt. Chief. The contrast between their appearances was dramatic. Luca was crushed, distracted, and dressed casually. Alfredo was confident, focussed, and decorated.

"What was it?" He asked the Chief.

"Oh, it was Midazolam...." He said, grimly. *"They believe it was... twenty-five milligrams."*

Luca shifted uncomfortably.

"Twenty-five?"

"Mmm. They said that you found her."

Luca nodded.

"It's good that you found her when you did."

"How is she?"

Alfredo gestured his head to the side, looking down the hall. Luca walked down the hallway, approaching distant chatter. He passed a set of bathrooms, arriving at a small medical room across from the large lab. He was greatly surprised to see Tera inside the room, standing, laughing with a couple of forensic assistants. She was dressed, her right arm displaying three bandages.

"How horrible!" Tera laughed uneasily.

"It's not the worst thing I've seen," one assistant bragged. Tera looked over at him through the doorway, then steadily looked back at the others. She looked guilty and pale. They all quieted down when they noticed Luca. One of the assistants cut off a medical bracelet from Tera's wrist and handed her a bottle of fizzy water. Luca looked incredibly cautious, as though talking to Tera was as delicate an operation as defusing a bomb. She walked over to him.

"Hi…" she said, before walking past him towards Alfredo. Luca opened his mouth to speak, but no words came out. He just stood there, in front of the door, watching as the Sgt. Chief and an assistant escorted Tera to the elevator.

Luca later joined Alfredo for a very late, very quiet lunch. The two of them sat in Alfredo's squad car outside the station, eating sandwiches from the nearby deli. Every now and then the two would look at each other, but that was about as far as the communication went until they finished eating.

"Eventually you're going to have to tell her," Alfredo said seriously. Luca crumpled up his sandwich paper and stuffed it into a flimsy plastic bag.

"She doesn't care about what I have to say," Luca replied. Alfredo looked at Luca before opening his door to get out.

"You might be surprised."

23

The memorial service was taking place at the Cathedral Basilica of Santa Maria Assunta. This tiny cathedral was a famous Foggia landmark, beloved by historians, older locals, and tourists. But it was tiny. Luca got a ride to the cathedral after changing into his uniform. He arrived quite early, but the place was already overflowing. Even though the event was designed to be private, and relatively intimate, hundreds of people were inside and out of the cathedral, passing out photos of the victims, memory candles, paper lanterns, and homemade bracelets that read *#UnitiPerFoggia*.

Members of the local church met in groups around the building to pray. A few media organizations made it through the local red tape to film brief snippets for the evening news; they didn't stick around long. Most of the seats inside were reserved for family and friends of the victims and survivors, but the organizers of the service did ask to have a few representatives of the emergency responders and police present, to honor them for their service. They were told to stand in the front of the church, bordering the pews.

The Sergeant joined the others from the station at the right side of the cathedral's nave. Six wooden caskets filled the small stage at the end of the cathedral. The atmosphere was dominated by the majestic sounds of the pipe organ and the smell of lilies and chrysanthemums.

Luca was surprised and encouraged to see the faces of agents Carlo Raggi and Massimo Chelli. Both men were standing proud in the line of police, donning their uniforms along with pairs of crutches. He hadn't seen them since before the shooting. They were among the first wave of policemen to arrive at the restaurant that night, and along with agent Ferraro, were the only police who came into physical contact with the shooter and lived to tell about it. But unfortunately, none of their testimonies were very helpful, since they only interacted with the man for about seven seconds before losing consciousness. Even so, they were proud to serve their city. Luca greeted them before taking his place.

Several church members from the Basilica donated their time to help organize the flow of traffic for the service, getting people to their seats in an orderly manner. He scanned the crowd and eventually saw Tera walk in, hand in hand with Maria. She looked better already, though still a bit weak. He watched them sit next to Carlos and Sig.ra. Di Maggio in the front row on the left. By four o'clock the place was absolutely packed, and the service began. The officiant stood in front of the people and read:

"My tears have been my food day and night, while they continually say to me, 'where is your God?' You number my wanderings; put my tears into Your bottle; are they not in your book? For you have delivered my soul from death, my eyes from tears, and my feet from falling. Those who sow in tears shall reap in joy."

The people responded with the Lord's prayer:

Padre nostro che sei nei cieli,
sia santificato il tuo nome;
venga il tuo regno,
sia fatta la tua volontà,
come in cielo così in terra.
Dacci oggi il nostro pane quotidiano,
rimetti a noi i nostri debiti,
come noi li rimettiamo ai nostri debitori
e non ci indurre in tentazione,
ma liberaci dal male.

Interspersed with more scripture and song, the service had brief moments to remember each of the six

Foggia victims from the shooting. Family members and friends were given an opportunity to read off short statements about who the person was, and what their life meant to them.

Among the six locals who were killed, there was Riccardo Di Maggio, the owner of *Fiore Dorato*. He was known by many for his wry smile and outgoing personality. He was a husband, a brother, and a father of three. There were Thomas and Stefano Esposito, brothers who were dining at the restaurant. There was Alessandro Marino, the owner of a pottery shop, who was sitting at the bar when the shooting began. Gioia Donini was a seamstress, a wife, a mother, and a grandmother of seven. Finally, there was Carlotta Duca, a member of *Fiore Dorato's* kitchen staff. Carlotta was only twenty and was caught in the crossfire while serving a table.

After the mass, family members lifted and carried out the six caskets, up, over their heads, as is traditionally done in these parts. Tera wondered about the nine names they didn't read off at the memorial. The Catholic church has the right to deny funerary rites to "manifest sinners" to avoid "public scandal among the faithful." But Rudolfo Garbazzi and his men were people too. They had lives. They had families. Who would remember them?

After the service, there was a free dinner for the families, friends, and survivors at the nearby town hall. Tera sat quietly with Maria amongst the many. Conversations were pretty hushed, most people were talking about the service, or sharing memories about those who had been killed. Apart from a few members of law enforcement, no one there knew about Tera's near-death experience. She had only told Maria that she had been feeling sick.

They left the dinner early and met with a group from their church, who gathered around Tera to pray. This prayer circle gave Tera a safe place to cry. It was not easy for her to let herself cry, but she was now learning how to be ok with that. She saw Matteo there with his family, chasing his nephews around the courtyard. She let him give her a hug.

Luca wasn't hungry, so he didn't stay for the dinner. But he didn't want to go home either. He was pretty sure of what would happen if he went back to work while it was still his day off, so he changed out of his uniform and stashed it in Alfredo's squad car. He sat outside the town hall, on the edge of a stone wall, and watched small groups of people pray and sing. This is where Tera spotted him, amongst the surrounding graffiti, the wind gently blowing his hair and clothing. Tera pulled on Maria's arm.

"Come on, I want you to meet someone," she said. The two of them walked over and looked up at him on the wall.

"Maria, this is Luca Conti, the man who saved my life."

Luca looked down at the two of them as Maria looked confusedly at Tera. He pushed himself off of the short wall, gracefully landing on his feet.

"*Buonasera,*" he said to Maria. He looked at Tera delicately.

"I'm not the only one who saved your life," he said, feeling leery. Maria ran up and shook his hand, effectively waking him out of his contemplative stupor.

"*Salve! Piacere di conoscerla!*"

Luca laughed a little, cracking a smile. Maria looked back at Tera.

"You didn't tell me he speaks English!"

Tera nodded briefly. She looked around pensively before eventually looking at Luca.

"Are you doing anything tonight?" she asked. "Because if you're not, we would love your company."

"And your car!" Maria added. Tera gave Maria a sour look, then looked at Luca hopefully.

"Ah, I see how it is," Luca said. "You two would use a man for his car."

Tera felt terrible inside, hearing him say that. But she knew he was kidding.

"No…" she said, "but I would pay him gas money for a sunset."

Luca looked at the sky,

"Where do you want to go? You're running out of daylight."

"West." Tera smiled.

Luca looked around the courtyard for a bit before nodding.

"Then we had better get walking." He motioned with his head for them to follow. It was about fifteen minutes to Luca's car, and another ten to drive out of Foggia. By the time they entered the country the sun was beginning to throw bright colors across the sky.

24

Tera and Maria insisted on sitting in the back, since they were paying for a "taxi ride." Leaving Foggia feels more like returning than leaving. Immediately that little black car became swallowed up by the lush green plots of surrounding farms. As far as the eye could see, it was endless gold and green, colors that only grew deeper and richer as the sky's pink and orange hues showed stronger and brighter. Tera felt at home in that contrast. It was a place you could dwell in for but a handful of time, chasing the sun to find rest in the comfort of its setting.

"See if you can catch it," Tera whispered to Luca, pointing at the brilliant horizon.

"Ok," he said, grinning, and pressed his foot down on the acceleration - which consequently threw the two young ladies back into their seats. Tera felt her heart race as the little black Audi shot ahead into the flat green farmland. Luca watched the dial climb. He knew how fast this machine could go, but being a responsible taxi driver, he decided not to push it past 200 km/hr. Maria and Tera started screaming in excitement, Maria shouting things that Tera couldn't translate. They sped along until the sun disappeared. Luca let up on the gas and they slowed to a more reasonable velocity.

"How far do you want to go?" he asked them. They were quickly approaching Lucera, zipping past barns, giant stacks of hay, and small orchards. If Tera had only had a few other things with her, she would have asked to go to Portugal, but as it was, she was already violating her order not to leave the city. She stared out the window at the mountains in the distance, fading slowly into the dusk.

"Can we go to the stars?" she asked softly.

"Ah yes, how far can this taxi go?" Maria echoed.

Luca scratched his head before reaching for his phone. They took their time and looped around Lucera, then took a side road off of SS17 into Pellegrino. Luca pulled over on the side of the road, nothing but flat farms on all sides. They all got out of the car. It was quiet, but for the sounds of crickets, the trains, and some distant traffic.

"Non so come, ma ce l'abbiamo fatta." Luca looked up at the night sky.

"Excellent taxi service. We shall give you a good review," Maria said.

They spent some time pointing out the constellations they knew. Luca could trace out Cassiopeia, Cepheus, and Draco. Tera could only go as far as the Big Dipper and Orion's Belt. Maria really blew them out of the water on this one; she knew her Serpens Caput and her Coma Berenices. Luca and Tera watched in awe as Maria pointed out every star from one side of the sky to the other.

"How do you know all of this?" Tera asked in amazement.

"Oh, I have a sky map on my ceiling." Maria smiled big. "I love the stars."

"Most people love the stars, Maria... you seem... obsessed."

Maria giggled with pride. Luca looked at her inquisitively.

"Maria, I am curious... Do you think volcanoes are interesting?" He asked it almost as a joke, but Maria excitedly affirmed that she did, and Tera shot Luca a knowing glance while Maria began to tell them about volcanoes on other planets.

"Can you see Venus or Mars?" Tera asked.

"Which are those?" Maria asked.

"Venere, e Marte," Luca translated.

"Ah, sì!" Maria pointed out Mars by the Taurus constellation. She said Venus must be below the horizon.

"So," Luca started, after a brief pause, "you are telling us that *Venere* will not rise until after *Marte* sets?"

"Yes... I think so," Maria responded, less confidently.

"Well, that makes sense," he replied.

"Oh? And how would you know this?" Maria asked, a little vexed.

"Personal experience..." he mumbled. Maria gathered that he wasn't talking about the stars anymore, so she didn't press him on it.

Every few minutes car headlights would appear in the distance, making their way between Lucera and Foggia. The unrelenting trains traveled frequently and swiftly at the edge of the horizon in both directions. There were so many things that each of them wanted to talk about, but none of them spoke of any of it. Not of the shooting, the memorial service, the past, the future - nothing. Just the stars.

Maria wanted to know how Luca saved Tera's life, or whatever that was about. Tera wanted to tell them about the man with the gun from the salon. Luca just wanted to know what was going on in Tera's head, and whether or not she was planning to hurt herself again.

Tera fell asleep in the car on the ride back, her head resting on Maria's shoulder. Maria woke her when they got back to her apartment. She helped her up and walked her into her place. Tera gave Maria a big hug, and a fifty Euro note to give to Luca.

"That's ridiculous," Maria told Tera, looking at the money. "He's not going to take that."

"Try," Tera said, before pushing her out and murmuring "*Buonanotte.*"

Maria had many unanswered questions, and may have led Luca on a wild goose chase around the city so that she could get answers before being dropped off. Out of sensitivity to Tera, Luca did his best to keep his secrets. He could dodge pretty well when he wanted to. Maria managed to get some information, though. Luca grew up Catholic. He was born in June. He did have family, but they were not close. In fact, from what Maria could gather, it sounded like they hated him. His mother was living with his older sister, and her husband, in Florence. He had brothers, but Maria couldn't get any information about them, much to her chagrin.

In the process of avoiding Maria's questions, Luca managed to learn a little about Tera's experience in the U.S., and the man there who ruined her life. Luca didn't know that the man responsible was still alive. Maria had assumed that as a cop, Luca already knew those details, but quickly shut her mouth when she realized he did not.

"Ok, If you can't remember where you live within the next thirty seconds, I'm going to drop you at the nearest bus stop," Luca told her firmly.

"Va bene, va bene..." Maria pointed up the road, quickly directing him to her address. She stuffed the Euro note into his cup holder just before getting out. She strutted back to her family's house and promptly called Tera. Tera was fast asleep, so she left a voicemail:

"Ciao Tera. Call me if you can't sleep, ok?"

25

Tuesday.

Tera woke up like a rock. Maybe it was the drugs still working out of her system, but she slept long and hard and somehow still felt terrible.

Part of yesterday's consequences included a particularly confusing series of questionings and an impromptu therapy session to determine that Tera was safe to be on her own. Unlike her counseling sessions with Dott.ssa Giuliani, these mental health professionals got right to the point. And then of course the Carabinieri wanted to know why she staged a break-in, and how she got the drugs. She couldn't remember.

Tera was determined to remain honest, but separating fact from fiction was tricky; she was mentally and physically screwed up by the sedative, and from what she could remember, she knew she didn't want to say too much. Yesterday morning was also emotionally confusing, since Tera was legitimately thrilled to be alive.

One night of sleep wasn't enough to fix her problems, but her mind was less foggy today. After staring at herself in her bathroom mirror for a while, Tera decided that she would pay Luca a visit before going to her afternoon counseling session. While their little trip last night helped patch things up, she still felt she owed him an explanation as he no doubt would want to know why she drugged herself. At the least, she could thank him for being there for her. For saving her life. And she also wanted her apartment keys back.

Tera was still walking toward the police station when she saw men in military uniforms entering and exiting the station's West entrance with boxes upon boxes, loading them into various black vehicles. She entered through the main door to immediately see two agents behind the glass window shouting at a tiny woman in a suit who remained unphased. Tera recognized the woman. It was Chief Inspector Greta Greco, the detective who was assisting the Chief Marshall Russo at her second interrogation.

After a minute, another State policeman entered the room behind the glass and pulled one of the two agents out. Soon Greta left the room as well, with the other agent, still yelling at her, in tow. Tera took a seat, watching the empty room through the glass, waiting for something else to happen. She could hear some shouting through the walls, but nothing clear enough to make out. Eventually, the hall door opened and Scraggy walked out. He saw Tera and threw his arms into the air. Without a word, he pointed at her, held up his index finger, and walked back through the door. Tera waited.

Minutes went by. Tera decided to text Maria. Looking at her contacts, she noticed some fake names had been added into her phone, including: "Mr. Sexy," "The Money" and "Your Best Man." She pondered this for a moment until she remembered that Luca and both Marcos had her phone for a few hours on Saturday. She would have to investigate this later, as she didn't recognize the numbers for any of the three contacts.

The hall door flew open, but instead of Scraggy, it was Chief Inspector Greco and a yelling cop. Greco had a bag on her shoulder, and when she walked to the front door, she stopped and looked at Tera.

"Ah!" She smiled, *"Perfetto."* Amidst the verbal bombardment, she opened her bag, took out a large sealed envelope, and handed it to Tera. Without any explanation she left the station, leaving the agent in the doorway to shout various creative insults - mostly involving pigs - out to the parking lot.

Scraggy came rushing into the lobby through the hall door, and tagged the yelling cop on the shoulder,

"L'abbiamo salvato," he said, before both men rushed back through the hall door which closed with a clang. Tera looked at the envelope. It had her name on it, written by hand. She looked around the empty waiting room and began to tear it open from the right-hand corner. She hadn't finished before Scraggy and the no-longer-yelling cop entered the lobby through a side entrance, pushing dolly carts full of boxes with looks of concern on their faces. They passed her by and again entered through the hall door.

She finished opening the envelope and slid out its paper contents. It had an official document letterhead from the *Divisione Unità Specializzate Carabinieri*. Roughly translated, the letter read that Tera was no longer under any investigation by the Foggia State Police. It said that the State's case surrounding the shooting at the restaurant had been dissolved. Her records will now be handled solely by the Carabinieri. As a result, there were now no outstanding charges against her, and she was once again free to travel outside the country. She stared in disbelief, and reread the document. "This can't be real," Tera thought.

Scraggy and the other police agent came through the side doors again with another set of boxes on dollies. Once more they proceeded to walk past her and through to the hall. But this time, shortly behind them, came Luca, also pushing a full dolly. When he saw Tera he stopped, so suddenly that he almost lost a box off the top of his stack. He smiled nervously, but then pushed the dolly to the side of the lobby, and rested one arm on top of a box.

"Ciao, bella," he said quietly, with a smile buried under concern. "You came at a hectic time. The government is confiscating everything... from your case."

Tera pointed at the boxes. "What are those?"

"These..." Luca patted a box, "were taken by mistake. They are not related to the investigation. But... we had to fight to keep them anyway. Just part of the politics." Still leaning on the stack, he smacked the top box and straightened his cap.

"Does that mean you caught the shooter?" she asked, excited.

"*Mah...*" Luca shrugged and looked pretty frustrated. "We don't know. But it's out of our hands now."

"So... Should I come back later?" she looked at the papers, then smiled back to Luca who bit the side of his hand before looking at the floor, then the wall, then back at her.

"Yeah."

She nodded slowly at him. Scraggy and the other cop came through the side door again and stopped between Sgt. Conti and Tera. Scraggy looking at Sgt. Conti,

"*Cosa... Hai le braccia corte?*" He waved his arm in disgust.

"*Zitto! Sei licenziato!*" Luca shouted back playfully, throwing both hands in the air before pushing his dolly onward through the hall door. The other agents followed after, murmuring under their breath. Tera took this opportunity to leave.

She walked with confidence and freedom to her counseling session that afternoon. She was certain that today she and Fabrizia would be talking about yesterday morning, but she didn't care. A tremendous burden had been lifted off of her shoulders.

While walking to the clinic, Tera noticed a small group of men ahead of her in an alley. One of the men looked her way, which was enough to make her feel uncomfortable, so she took a turn down another street. She could take a detour and still be on time.

She made her way out of the small winding alleys to a more populated street. Feeling paranoid, she took some time to look around her, and after a block she noticed a bald man looking her way from the other side of the street, walking in parallel with her. She took a break at a bench to check out her foot, still healing from her self-brutalization over the weekend. Running from that security guard hadn't helped it heal any. The man across the street stopped to light a cigarette. Tera kept on walking; the man in turn did likewise. Tera, feeling suddenly bold, started to jog a little, and then to run, tearing through crosswalks and plowing through women holding grocery bags. She stopped after a minute, her foot once again throbbing. She looked to the other side of the street. Somehow the bald man had kept up. She was now very close to her destination and nervously pressed onward.

She soon entered the clinic lobby and immediately asked Tiziano at the desk about their building's security. He slowly asked, "*Va tutto bene?*" She walked around the small lobby in an antsy manner, two others who were waiting in the seating area looking up concernedly.

"It's probably nothing…I'm sure everything is fine," she said to him in English. He didn't understand what she said. She sat down by the others and played an imaginary keyboard on her lap. Soon after, her phone started to ring. Her phone was telling her that "The Money" was calling.

"Hello?" she answered, incredulously.

"Tera, this is Federico Russo. I need a moment of your time."

Tera let out a slight laugh. Whatever Marco and Marco had done to her phone, she was not expecting the Chief Marshall to be "The Money." She spoke quietly, directing her face away from the others.

"Hi, yeah. I mean, yes. Yes, sir. How may I help you?"

"Excellent. We need you to come to the Command Station immediately."

"I'm in a counseling session right now..."

"You will need to reschedule that for another time. We need you here as soon as possible. We are sending you a car. Where is your current location?"

She had to ask Tiziano for the address. Two minutes later a black SUV that read "Carabinieri" on the doors was waiting for her outside the clinic. Was this it for her? Was this her arrest? It had all seemed too good to be true - probably because it was never true. She walked outside. A man in a black uniform got out and opened the back door for her. She climbed in, and they started to move. The man in the front seat turned around, a gun pointed at her face.

26

"What!? Are you serious!?" she screamed. A man next to her grabbed her arm. It was the man from the hair salon.

"No, no, no! What is wrong with you people!" She started flailing and kicking everywhere, beyond frustrated. Struggling, she continued,

"I did every stupid thing you frickin' jerks demanded and you still have the nerve..."

"Calm down!" the man next to her yelled, grabbing her arms, trying to force handcuffs onto her. She put up a great fight, twisting spastically for several seconds. She was able to kick the man hard in the face with her "good" foot. He let out a loud "Oof!"

She tried in vain to open the car door from the inside. The man in the front with the gun was pretty useless. He just sat there and watched. Tera thought about grabbing the gun, but figured that wouldn't end well. She continued to kick and squirm.

"A little help here, please?" the man in the back shouted, holding his nose, warding off Tera's kicks with his other hand. The vehicle screeched to a halt. Tera was thrown forward in the seats, hitting her head on the inside of the door.

"Son-of-a..!" she hollered. They opened the door and dragged her into an alley.

"We won't kill you if you don't..." Whatever. She wasn't listening to them. She was WAY beyond done with this crap. She bit the leg of the man with the gun. He wasn't expecting that. She crawled at an insane speed, past their legs, got standing, and ran like never before. She was too slippery for their grasp to hold her, and she was flying now. She heard someone running behind her, and heard the car accelerating. She didn't immediately know where she was, but she figured she would be able to survive this if she could get near other people. There was no time to make a phone call. Not yet.

She turned left to a skinny alley, hoping a Jeep Grand Cherokee wouldn't fit behind her. They hadn't tried shooting at her yet, which was encouraging. She didn't dare take the time to look back. She came to a split in the alley. She took another left. The man running behind her sounded closer than before. She sprinted with every bit of energy she had. At the end of the block, she looked to her left and saw their SUV, backing up quickly at the end of the path, half a block away, getting ready to turn towards her. To her right, she saw her freedom: a busy street.

She bolted. It wasn't far. But it was just far enough: the SUV caught up to her. She hugged the side of the alley, and the car rushed past her, stopped suddenly, and the doors flew open. Three men in black uniforms leaped out, guns in hand, aimed not at Tera, but behind her. She collapsed. The man chasing her rounded the corner; he saw the wall of Carabinieri, and quickly changed course. Two of the policemen pursued, shouting,

"*Fermo! Fermo!*"

The third Carabiniere quickly collected Tera into the SUV.

She was pretty banged up. Her knees were badly scraped, now bleeding through her slacks. Her arms and palms were scratched up a little - not bad, but well on their way to being colorfully bruised. Her head was sore, and her foot was in excruciating pain. It was all she could do to catch her breath. The driver was talking continuously on his radio. After a few seconds, they could hear shots being fired. It wasn't much longer before a handful of cops on motorcycles zoomed past them, sirens screaming. Then, finally, an ambulance.

She rode in the back with a paramedic and two Carabinieri. They put a blanket around her. She shook their hands, thanking all of them for their service. It bothered her that she was getting used to this kind of thing.

Instead of the hospital, they took her to the Carabinieri Provincial Command Main Station. Russo greeted her inside a small medical center. She sat on a gurney, a nurse treating her knees and legs, wrapping them in a stretchy gauze. Her pants had been removed, a cloth draped across her lap. Another medical assistant was taking her blood pressure. Russo stood nearby, looking away, out of respect for Tera's privacy.

"You are truly an impressive woman," Russo said, "to have escaped in the way you did. We thought we were acting quickly, but they beat us to you."

"Who are those guys?" Tera asked, frustrated.

"We are still determining that. Organized crime has many forms."

"I recognized one of them," Tera turned towards Russo, pushing herself up on the gurney. One of the nurses gently pushed Tera back down while another started to look at her foot.

"He threatened me at gunpoint in a hair salon last week. Told me to shut up about the shooter's identity."

Russo snapped his fingers at one of the men in the hall.

"Chiamate un artista forense. Adesso!"

The man hurried off.

"And I did. I actually know what the shooter looks like. I can identify him. The State Police had his picture."

"That won't be necessary. You have been informed," Russo asked, "that the State Police will no longer be involved in this ongoing investigation?"

"Yeah," Tera said, "but, why? Did you already catch the shooter?"

"No. He is no longer our primary concern. We suspect corruption within the Foggia State Police unit," he said calmly.

"For your safety, *Signorina*, you must refrain from giving any additional information to the State Police."

Tera nodded with an affirmative "mmhmm." She tried not to make too much noise while the nurse tended to her foot. He was being gentle, but it was very sensitive, and she was ticklish too, which made it even more uncomfortable. She had also refused to take any of the pain medication that they offered.

"Why are they coming after me?" Tera asked.

"Perhaps you can help us answer that." Russo responded. "We know that whoever called you on Saturday morning left a voicemail. Care to tell us about that?"

Tera thought about it for a moment. Did the Carabinieri need to know that the shooter had been in her apartment? The gunman from the salon wasn't leaving her alone as promised. She couldn't care less about keeping his secret now.

"Yeah…" she started. "That was the shooter from *Fiore Dorato*. He was calling to help me... to help me protect him."

"Then your kidnappers may have been aware of this contact. It's possible they want to use you to get to the shooter."

"But why?" Tera asked, flopping her arms down onto the medical bed. "Why would they force me to protect him, and then want to do that?"

Russo paused for a moment.

"Perhaps motivations have changed on their end." A man came running into the medical center and spoke softly to Russo before departing again. Russo looked calm.

"Can you please hide me somewhere?" Tera started, "Stick me in a safe house until this gets figured out?"

Russo nodded. "If you like. Or," he paused. "If you're willing to comply, we might be able to use you to help bring all of this to an end."

Tera didn't like the sound of that at all. She would rather hide in a box for a week and let the professionals handle this. The nurse was now inspecting her head, which was good because there was likely something wrong with it by now. Despite everything, she was curious. She looked at Russo.

"How?"

27

After they finished cleaning her up they got her dressed in some new clothes, which almost fit. Then she spent a good deal of time trying to describe the man from the salon to a forensic sketch artist, who was able to do a pretty good job. Afterward, they sat her down in a small conference room with Russo, Greco, Napolitano, and two others that Tera didn't recognize.

"Can you guarantee I won't be killed?" Tera apprehensively scanned their faces.

"Chances are in your favor," Russo said.

"They would surely have killed you already if they wanted to do that," Napolitano added.

"I don't know about this…" Tera fidgeted around in her seat, staring back at the Lieutenant, "What if they're smarter than you?"

Napolitano looked greatly offended. Tera wondered whether or not he was single.

"Perhaps I am wrong," he eyed Tera with a dramatic face, *"But I received the impression yesterday that you are not opposed to the idea of dying."*

"Andrea," Russo snapped at him. *"Be nice."*

"What should I do if I am kidnapped again?" Tera asked, seriously concerned.

"Act natural," Greta said. *"And be patient."*

"Wherever they take you, we will be right behind you," added Russo.

"Should I answer their questions?" She looked around the room at the five of them.

"Not unless you have to," Napolitano said.

"What if they torture me?" Tera's eyes grew wide as she thought about this.

"It shouldn't even come close to that," Russo responded calmly.

Tera rolled her fingers across the top of the table.

"*Ohimè...*" she sighed, looking at them with a face full of worry. She thought about the man that she kicked in the face. And the man whose leg she bit. She didn't want to see them again. But she didn't want to live in fear of them for the rest of her life either.

They put so many tracers on Tera, she wondered if she had any privacy left. They installed a micro-beacon on to her bottom-right molar, which she was sure she would swallow. They fitted another one under her fingernail - which was not fun. Her stud earrings had something in them too. No microphones or cameras, from what she understood, but still, she felt like a walking piece of technology. Her phone was compromised as well, as were her sandals and her coat. The only thing they didn't wire up was the gun. They gave her a few different options for that. Tera wasn't used to concealed carry. She tried a few different types of holsters before giving up.

"There's no way this is going to help if I'm trying to get kidnapped." She looked at the two men in blue in front of her. Of course, they didn't understand why she felt uncomfortable stuffing a gun in her bra - they were men. She could maybe have done this with some practice, but as it stood, she preferred to have her own gun - in her hands. Any weapon she had now probably could and would be used against her. She thought about this again later when she strapped another knife to her leg. She really liked the knives they had. Knives are thin, and hide under clothing better than a gun.

They told her to act natural, but she felt like a moving target leaving the station. She was so uncomfortable, between the gauze, the knives, the bugs, and the very idea of what they were doing. She kept waiting for a car to drive up and usher her inside, or a group of strangers on the sidewalk to surround her and carry her off on their shoulders. She wanted to stand in the middle of a piazza and hold her arms out, close her eyes, and just wait for it to happen already.

She ended up in a bar. Maybe a drink would calm her down. She ordered a white russian, even though it wasn't a Monday. Tera must have looked distraught because three different guys took turns trying to cheer her up. She ignored all of them and watched the World Fencing Championships on the televisions instead. She thought about where she should go. Visiting friends would only put them in danger. Going home was... boring. She thought about Luca. He still had her key. She looked at her phone. It was only 6 pm. She ordered another white russian before leaving.

Well, she should have let one of those three guys buy her food because she was definitely tipsy when she left the bar. This was not ideal, or was it? She could still walk in a straight line, but now she felt strangely clouded and happy. It took about fifteen minutes to get to the police station. This would be easy, just march in, get the key, then get kidnapped.

She paused outside the door. She still had enough wit about her to know that she wasn't fully in her right mind, and suddenly this bothered her enough to hold herself back. She sat down on the pavement at the top of the steps by the front door, leaning against a glass transom window. If she didn't care so much about her lungs, now would have been a great time for a cigarette.

Inside, two police agents were scratching their heads, looking at her through the windows. She was becoming pretty well known around this place by now, so it's no surprise they informed their Sergeant about her. Tera heard a tapping on the window behind her. She turned around and looked up to see four policemen crowded at the window, smiling and waving down at her. She turned back around and continued to stare at the State Police Headquarters parking lot. This was now seeming like a really bad idea. Why was she here? She could have just called him, and had him meet her somewhere. He could have met her at the bar. Then she could have gotten another drink.

Luca walked into the lobby, scattering the cops away from the window. He opened the front door, and leaning against it, looked at Tera.

"Isn't life terrible?" she said, still staring at the parking lot. "You try so hard to do everything right, but in the end, it doesn't even matter. You still end up completely powerless."

Luca squinted at her for a minute.

"Rough day?"

"You don't, I don't… you don't even know." She shook her head. He nodded slowly at her, and looked around, thinking.

"Can I get you some water?" He pointed inside. She looked up at him and nodded. He gave her his hand and helped her up. She followed him through the hall door, down the hallway into his office. He kept the door open. She took off her jacket and sat on the couch. He gave her a glass of water and sat down next to her. He looked at her, half amused, half concerned. She drank it leisurely, trying to remember why she was there.

"So," she looked at Luca, "how are you?"

He smiled.

"I'm glad to see you."

"Oh, that's nice to hear," she said, drinking more water. She opened her mouth to start a sentence three different times, each time realizing she couldn't talk to him about that particular thing. He was starting to look a little frightened behind his smile.

"What did you have?" he finally asked, wondering if she was on something stronger than alcohol.

"More than enough I guess… may I please have some more water?"

Luca deftly slid off the couch and refilled her glass. He stood there for a moment before also handing her half a sandwich.

"Please eat this." It was the rest of his dinner, but she needed it more than he did. She looked at it.

"You're always so kind to me." She took a big bite. Luca rubbed the back of his neck and sat down again.

"I do know what it's like," Luca began, "to feel powerless." Tera looked at him and took another bite of the sandwich.

"You watch your life get destroyed, and just when you think you've pushed out all the chaos, it comes back to your door." He stared into his carpet. Tera stopped eating and studied him.

"You really do know what it's like, don't you."

Luca looked at Tera, with regret behind his eyes, but his look shifted to one of sympathy. He looked at his desk.

"I've read your file…" he said, unsure if talking about this was a good idea or not. Tera poked at the remaining bit of sandwich and drank some more water.

"Do you have it here?"

Luca gave a nod.

"Could I see it?" she asked. "I'm curious."

Luca walked over to the desk and opened a deep drawer full of files. Tera's gaze fell on some chess pieces that hid next to his desk lamp. She wondered who would win if they played. Luca flipped through the files and pulled hers out, tapped it on the desk twice.

"Are you sure you want to look at this?" He looked at her seriously.

She had already made a few bad decisions today. What was one more.

"Yeah, I'm sure." She stuffed the rest of the sandwich in her mouth; stood up; stepped forward; took the folder; opened it. Her mouth full, she slowly chewed and swallowed her past along with the food. It had several photos of her - from before... and after; every driver's license and passport. It had info on her work history; her gun registration; her health records. It had her old addresses from the States and some records of recently purchased plane tickets.

Honestly, a lot of the file was pretty boring. It was mostly black and white boxes with words typed in at slightly different levels of alignment; Tera found it cumbersome to look at. Until she got to the second half of the file.

There was nothing in there about the shooting, but they had an incident report from yesterday morning. There was a photo of her shoulder, and another of the syringe. There was an incident report from Friday night, with a photo of the broken window. Finally, there was a lengthy crime report from the US. It was the only part of her file that was in English. It had a photo of the man who killed her husband

and sister. She didn't read anything from that report. Just looked at the photo.

Luca looked at her silently.

"I went to see him," she pointed at the man in the picture, "a couple different times. My sister made me promise that I would try to see him. Our parents died when I was in college, so Dani was the one I looked up to, you know. She helped me get through the rest of school, get a job, plan my wedding... She only lived for a few days after she was shot." She set the open file down on the desk, still looking at the photo of the man. "So after everything... I went to see him. And I forgave him... for what he did." Luca stood still and marveled at her.

"It was the most freeing thing I've ever done," she said. "I actually became friends with his mother." She looked at Luca with a slight smile. "We still write to each other, now and then. And she was the one who encouraged me to travel, you know. She told me I had no reason not to live a wonderful life." She closed the file.

"Why did you try to kill yourself?" Luca asked quietly. He looked concerned for Tera, but also looked hurt. Tera's smile quickly disappeared. She wasn't sure how to answer that. They could both hear people walking in the hall. Luca walked over to the door and closed it softly.

"You gave me your key... you knew I would find you." He looked at her, calm, but upset. "Why would you do that to me?"

Tera wanted to tell him everything, but she remembered Russo's instructions. If there was someone in the State Police leaking information, then it wasn't safe to tell Luca about that night. She thought about what she could still say without lying.

"Because I didn't want to die... and I trust you." She started to feel embarrassed, thinking about what that must have been like for him to find her. "I'm so sorry..." she whispered. "I know I hurt... a lot of people."

Luca took off his cap and hung it on the rack by the door. He unclipped his radio from his uniform and belt, and set it on the desk.

"What are you doing?" she puzzled. He leaned against the wall with his hands in his pockets.

"You said it yourself last night... that I saved your life." He gazed at her and raised an eyebrow. *"Maybe you wish to thank me?"*

Tera was pretty sure that she wasn't getting her key back today. Maybe it would be best if she had her locks changed instead. She did put this guy through a lot, but she didn't owe him anything. And she wasn't about to let his Italian charm get the best of her. Even so, seeing him there, she felt drawn to him. She walked towards him slowly, his eyes locked in on hers. She got real close, slid her hands above his, onto the sides of his belt, and leaned in. Moving her face to his, she brushed his clean-shaven cheek with her lips before whispering in his ear,

"Thank you."

Being so close to him, Tera thought he smelled pleasantly like coffee. She gently kissed his neck, then quickly grabbed her jacket and got out of there.

28

He watched her walk down the hall for a few seconds before calling after her.

"*Signorina*,"

She stopped and turned. Luca was smiling at the floor between them before looking up at her.

"If you don't mind, I would like to ask you some... quick questions about Sunday... before you go." He grabbed his radio and his hat, and stepped out into the hall, motioning for her to follow him with a nod and a smirk. They stepped into a small conference room with white plastic tables and metal chairs. Luca finished clipping on his radio while he walked over to a small box of files sitting on the table.

"Please sit anywhere." He waved his hand around the room. Tera took a seat at the opposite side of the small table, wondering what to expect.

"Sorry about this..." he said, pulling out some paperwork. "Yesterday happened so quickly, and some things never got sorted before the memorial. Then today, they took so many of our case files... you saw earlier." He looked over at her. "And I figure, with you already here, we can get some of this straightened out now. Then we will not have to worry about it later."

"What do you... need?" Tera asked, watching Luca spread out a number of documents near her.

"A few of our facts don't line up. Yesterday you told us that you opened your apartment window, staging a break-in so that your... death wouldn't be considered... a suicide... *si?*" He looked at her quickly, before looking back at the paperwork.

"But the medical staff reported that you opened the window after, not before, you injected yourself with the drug. Do you remember which it was?"

"No, that's not right..." Tera adjusted herself in her chair. "I..." she paused, trying to remember. "I would have pushed the bench beneath the window, opened it, and then after that, injected myself in the shoulder. I know I threw the needle in the trash and then locked myself... in the bathroom." She looked at the table. That seemed right, but she was suddenly doubting herself.

"And then I sat there, and waited," she added.

Luca wrote something down and crossed something out.

"What time did you do this?"

"About..." Tera looked at Luca, "why?"

Luca clicked his pen.

"Can you remember?"

Tera looked around shiftily.

"No." She tried not to think about it too much. Her memory was pretty foggy, and that was working to her advantage at the moment.

"The medical staff have indicated that you were unconscious for almost eleven hours."

"That sounds right," she said.

"But that can't be right, if you were still awake after four in the morning to open your window, which is what the security cameras show."

Tera didn't say anything, but her eyes opened wider at the word "cameras."

"That would mean that you were only unconscious for…" Luca checked the papers.

"Seven hours, at the most." He looked at her. "Which would not be possible with twenty-five milligrams of Midazolam in your system."

She continued to say nothing, although twenty-five sounded like a large number to her.

"Unless you didn't have twenty-five milligrams in your system, but then why would forensics have detected that? Do you know how much you injected yourself with?"

Tera remained silent. Luca looked very puzzled.

"If what you said is correct, and you opened the window before…" Luca looked a little worried, "then you would have injected yourself with less than fifteen milligrams, sometime after four or five in the morning."

Tera looked at Luca briefly, then down at the table. She didn't count on the police doing the math. Luca blinked a few times, feeling the space between them grow.

"Tera?" He looked at her. She was starting to fidget. "You truly didn't want to kill yourself… did you." Luca looked at the papers, his suspicion and concern increasing every moment. Tera needed to do something quick if she wanted to stop this ball from rolling. She could pretend that she thought fifteen was enough to kill her, but she didn't want to lie to Luca.

"How do you know the cameras were right? Maybe they got the time wrong?" That was a stupid thing for her to ask.

"No..." Luca froze. *"These times are not wrong..."*

"Oh..." Tera sucked her lips into her teeth and let out a "hmm..." looking nervously around at the table. Staying for this little questioning session was a very big mistake. Luca tapped his hand on the paper and began to look around the room seriously. They remained quiet for a long few seconds. Tera wondered what would happen if she bolted out of the room.

"So you did this... what... because you wanted to get into the forensics lab...?"

Tera started to freak out inside. Her breathing changed, and she became visibly worried. Luca noticed.

"That means... you lied to us before," he said, piecing things together. "At the old apartment. You lied about something."

He looked at Tera, his face now filling with what looked like fear. "You were very convincing," he rested his hand near his gun, "Why... why would you lie about that night?" Tera remained sitting, staring at the table, looking like a guilty child caught in the act of disobeying. She thought about what she should do. Then she remembered something comforting. She didn't have to do anything, because the State Police didn't have access to any of the forensic evidence from the shooting anymore. They didn't have anything to hold over her head. They couldn't even pursue this if they wanted to. The Carabinieri were on her side, so this would just be a matter of time.

"Was it the shooter? From the restaurant?" Luca slowly put his fingers on the handle of his gun. His voice was hushed.

"Is he the one who called you? Are you working with him?" He waited a long time before yelling, "Tera! Why won't you talk to me?" As hurt turned to caution, he mumbled at her under his breath, *"Why else would he go to you? Why else would you lie?"*

"Um…" Tera started, now feeling a little more annoyed than afraid. His expression changing from caution to anger,

"Tera… can I trust you?"

Tera wanted to reply "maybe," but she really didn't want that on any official record, so she shrugged, lightly tossed her hands in the air, and kept her mouth shut.

"Ok," Sgt. Conti began to nod, *"Alzati."* He slid his Beretta out of its holster, keeping his finger on the safety. Tera remained seated, now looking around the room. *"I said GET UP,"* he lifted his gun, waving it at Tera. She stood up and calmly walked around the table away from him.

"Your gun is not loaded," she said calmly, and began to walk to the door. The *Sovrintendente* looked down at his gun in confusion before looking in horror as Tera took his pistol's magazine out of her pants pocket and set it on the table, calmly picking up her jacket and walking out of the room. She was just being playful with him in the office; she didn't want to put him in any danger. She did feel weird though, throwing ammo at him now that he was aiming his gun at her. He hastily grabbed the mag and loaded his gun, moving quickly around the table and out of the room after her. Tera slowly walked down the hall, her jacket under her arm, and her hands in her pockets. Sgt. Conti's heart was beating fast, trying to understand.

"Romano!" he called loudly, *"Rinforzo! Adesso, adesso!"* He aimed his gun at Tera's back. Scraggy came bursting through the doors, looking every which way in confusion, he was joined shortly after by two others.

"Sovrintendente?" Scraggy looked at them.

"Ferma!" Luca finally shouted at Tera. She stopped, and dropped her jacket, lifting her hands. She turned around sheepishly. The Sergeant looked at Scraggy,

"Arrestatela!"

He lowered his gun and watched in disbelief as agent Romano pushed a very compliant Tera into the hallway wall, and cuffed her hands behind her back. Another agent emptied her coat pockets of her cellphone, keys, and some chapstick.

"You need a reason to arrest me. I'd love to know what that is." Tera said this calmly to *Agente* Romano while he cuffed her. Scraggy looked back at Luca.

"False testimony given to law enforcement... Probable cause of... conspiracy with a killer at large." They marched her down a few halls that she had yet to see in that building. These were the ones that led to the cell blocks. After walking past a security guard at a desk, they entered the empty room of cells. Agent Romano opened the old metal door, and Tera calmly walked in and sat on the small cushioned bench. Sgt. Conti stood in front of the cell, looking in at Tera through the old off-white bars as agent Romano locked it shut.

Tera looked up at Luca. It didn't matter. She was able to get the sponge when she was in the forensics lab. They made it so easy for her. They left her alone. The doors were unlocked. No cameras in that part of the building. She'd found the bloody thing in a sealed paper bag, which she conveniently lost down the toilet. She made it back to the hospital bed and fell asleep before they came back to check on her. Her only mistake must have been opening her window too late, not thinking about the cameras.

"Non capisco…" Agent Romano looked at the Sergeant, waving his hands. Luca looked silently at Scraggy until he left the room with the others. Luca looked back at Tera.

"Why you?" he asked.

Tera let out a small laugh,

"I often ask the same question!" She lifted her cuffed hands into the air and dropped them into her lap, smiling at the cell walls.

"I have to keep you here," Luca said, angrily, "until I know why that shooter was coming back... to you." He fit his gun back in its holster. She could tell he was really mad. "And if you'd like to help me figure that out," he walked closer to the cell door, "then maybe I'll let you go."

"You know," she looked straight into his angry, brown eyes, "this is the safest I've felt in a long time."

He said nothing, but walked away without a second look. Tera took a big breath and let out a huge sigh of relief. She wasn't sure what would happen next, but for some reason, she felt free.

29

Luca stormed down the hall, blasting through the others, a force not to be dealt with. He opened his office door, slamming it into the wall before it closed shut. Seething, he took out his phone and hurriedly searched for a contact. He dialed the *Maresciallo Capo*, but was given the *Tenente*.

"*Tell me,*" answered Napolitano.

"*No. I don't want to talk to you. I need to speak to Chief Marshall Russo.*"

"*Russo is a very busy man. What could possibly be so urgent?*"

"*I need access to the files that you took from us this morning.*"

"*Sergeant Conti, you know that is not possible. Once a decision of ours has been made, it cannot be undone simply because...*"

"*But this is of great importance, we have a suspect in custody. This is new information about the mass murderer and possib...*"

"*Suspect? In the Golden Flower shooting? You are not authorized to continue pursuing that case.*"

"*Then perhaps I can assist you. I have good reason to believe that her previous testimony, the greatest contributing evidence that we have, is invalid. She could be dangerous. I need to see the forensics results from...*"

Napolitano shouted emphatically, interrupting Conti,

"If a case is withdrawn from the State Police, then you are no longer entitled to that investigation! You have no authority to hold a suspect in custody for a..."

"I have every right to hold a suspect in custody if I have probable cause!"

"You arrested the girl? On what charges?"

"Her testimony is in conflict with itself. She admits to having lied on the record, and she attempted assault on police authority. Manipulation of law enforcement resources, possible tampering with evidence."

"Assault?"

"Disarming a policeman."

"Who on your staff is so reckless to allow a little girl to disarm them?

Luca said nothing.

"Are we going to work together on this, or not?"

Luca finally added.

"You and I have no reason to work together, Sergeant. We will take the girl off your hands and look into this ourselves."

"Your feeble ancestors will take her off my hands. You have no authority to remove her from our custody."

That really ticked the Lieutenant off.

"If you think I will give you even a small piece of what you are asking for, then you can go to hell like a pig! We will have someone there shortly to take the girl."

"I'd love to see you attempt that!" Conti shouted back, "You can't ignore the law, and I will NOT ignore State crimes!"

"*State crimes should be treated by the State,*" the young *Tenente* retorted, "*but it doesn't matter, because this isn't a State level case! Your case with the girl is CLOSED!*" He hung up the phone.

Conti shouted curses at the wall. The other police agents peered down the long hall towards Conti's office, as the muffled yelling carried through the door. Romano looked at the others, pulled up his belt, and strutted back to his position. The others slowly followed suit.

Less than an hour later the battle on the phone brought its ugly face to the doors of the police headquarters. The Carabinieri marched through the lobby, similarly to how they had done earlier that day, pushing their crisp light-blue uniforms and shiny white belts into the offices and corridors of the police station. But this time the State Police were ready to put up a fight. Despite the military strength of the Carabinieri, Sgt. Conti's words were correct. They didn't have the authority to take Tera.

The two parties of Italian law enforcement were about ready to wrestle each other to the floor when Sgt. Chief Cociarelli finally showed up. He walked calmly into the tumultuous conference room where the two shades of blue were fighting it out, and set a piece of paper on the table. It was communication from the *Prefetto*. It shut everyone up. *Tenente* Napolitano picked up the paper and read it. He swore, then led the rest of his team out of the station, retreating back to their base in the darkness of the night.

Conti and Cociarelli looked at each other. Conti kicked over a chair, harsh echoes filling the room. He paced. The others looked on, exhausted. This didn't feel like a victory. The hours were growing late, and a few agents had stayed overtime for this. Cociarelli dismissed the agents from the room, relieving the tired policemen, and instructing the ones who were just beginning their shifts. He brought Luca into his office, and they stood in silence. Alfredo's office had a large grandfather clock that ticked noticeably every second, and chimed softly every fifteen minutes.

"You need to rest."

"I can't go home."

"Get a hotel. Stay with a friend. Dammit, Luca. You can sleep at my house if you need to. But you can't stay here. Not like this. You need to take care of yourself."

The worn-out Sergeant sat in the green armchair, took off his police cap, and put his face in his hands.

"You have no idea how lucky you are Alfredo, to have Marta," he despaired.

"I do not envy your situation, my boy. You are a victim of cruel circumstances."

Luca sat up and blinked hard. He gave a heavy sigh and looked to his captain with sad eyes.

30

Wednesday.

Tera slept oddly well in the cell that night. It was the best she had slept in weeks. It was like waking up from a long, strange dream. She felt so refreshed and clear-headed, despite the stale smell of her surroundings. They woke her up when they came to bring her breakfast. It was agent Ferraro, with the pretty eyes. He brought her the Italian equivalent of stale bread and water, which was a buttery croissant and water. The croissant was pretty good. Ferraro didn't stick around very long, so she didn't get a chance to ask if she could make a phone call. If they would let her, she knew who she would call. She would call Maria, and let her know that she was feeling so much better about everything in life now that she was in jail.

Meanwhile, in the screwed up halls of Italian justice, the Carabinieri discussed what to do about Tera. The Lieutenant was skimming through thick books with a collection of other agents, trying to find a loophole in the law. Anything that they could use to get Tera back.

"Maybe a bargain is our best option," he said.

"I will not risk compromising any more information, to retrieve our bait," said Russo.

"We will not catch any fish if our bait remains in someone else's tackle box." The Lieutenant closed his book emphatically.

"I don't understand. Why can't we transfer the suspect into our custody?" asked another young Carabiniere.

"Because," replied Napolitano, *"the suspect isn't being held for a crime related to the Golden Flower investigation. She is being held for a crime against the pig-damned State."*

Russo passed a copy of Tera's crime report to the young agent. Luca might have been furious when he locked her up, but he was still clever enough to only arrest Tera - on paper - for disarming him. It would be another four days before Tera would be required to see a judge, and with video surveillance as evidence, the State could hold her for up to twenty years, just for this one crime.

Luca also took care to promptly inform the U.S. Consulate of Tera's complex situation, so *Tenente* Napolitano spent most of that morning trying to delicately deal with Mrs. Flora Amenta, whom the Consulate sent back to Foggia to "ensure proper treatment of the U.S. suspect in accordance with the law." So in addition to everything else, the Carabinieri now had unwanted foreign eyes on them.

"Can we hire a defense lawyer on her behalf?"

"No. Nothing public. We want to stay out of court."

"Can we bribe the judge for a transfer order?"

The others looked at each other uneasily for a few seconds, some actually pondering this suggestion.

"Are you an idiot? Of course we cannot do that." Russo's voice boomed through the conference hall, followed by heavy sighs.

Greta Greco entered the room.

"I have our solution," she declared, under a tired smile. *"Although it does not inspire the most confidence in our investments."* She set down a flimsy collection of papers, haphazardly fastened together. *"I'm afraid that what I've found is disturbing... but it should be sufficient to loosen their grip."*

She slid the papers to Russo while the others began to stir excitedly.

"We will be transferring her into custody here?" he asked, taking the papers.

"No," she shook her head quickly and adjusted her slim glasses, *"but we should be able to get her out."*

Tera looked up at the skinny white camera on the wall, pointed directly at her. She made faces at it, hoping someone, somewhere, might get a laugh out of it. She sat on the bunk with her feet up, legs crossed, staring at the strange Italian jail-toilet. It had a short privacy wall, but was still fairly exposed. She was sure that these cells were not constructed with women in mind. She looked back at the camera, bouncing her cuffed hands on her lap. Tera still had knives and gauze wrapped around her legs. *Agente* Romano never bothered to frisk her, whether out of neglect, or fear of Luca... or some other reason.

She heard the door open, out of view. Slow footsteps approached her cell. It was the Sgt. Chief.

"*Signorina* Laurito.*"*

Tera sat up, looking at the serious man in his decorative uniform. He easily commanded her respect. She wasn't sure why, but she felt that Alfredo was on her side. He gave her a look that seemed to indicate either trust or admiration. *Ispettore Capo* Greco entered shortly thereafter. Greta sighed when she saw her. Tera felt embarrassed. Tera had one job, and somehow she managed to wind up here. She was expecting to have to answer questions, but instead, the Sgt. Chief opened the cell door, and ushered Tera out. Together the three of them walked out of the cellblock, and into the room outside. The skeptical guard at the door unlocked Tera's cuffs, and the four of them proceeded to the interrogation room. Tera hated this room. But this time they didn't ask her any questions. She watched as the tiny detective and prudent Sgt. Chief signed documents in almost total silence.

Before parting ways in the hall outside, Alfredo gave Tera a look that seemed full of compassion, if not condolence. In the Police station lobby, Tera was once again handed her jacket and an envelope. Greta accompanied Tera out the door to a sleek Carabinieri vehicle. Once inside, Tera looked at the tiny woman, with a timid grin.

"*Grazie*..." She was a bit impressed. *"Thank you for getting me out."*

"It wasn't easy. Whatever you shared with them caused enough damage to demand a compromise. Luckily we had something to offer that wouldn't spoil our efforts."

"I did not intend to tell them anything... They figured it out." Tera felt foolish, giving excuses.

"To your knowledge, are the State Police aware of the man who threatened you at the hair salon? Or of your kidnapping?"

"No," Tera replied.

"*Bene*," Greta sighed. She straightened out her pencil skirt, looking out the window at the State Police Headquarters fading into the distance.

"What did you have to give them, to get me out?" Tera asked. Greta looked at Tera for a moment.

"In exchange for your charges being dropped, we provided them with our database of forensic evidence related to all of the incidents that you were involved with."

"Wha... *veramente?*" Tera was quite surprised, *"Why would you do that?"*

"To prove we have nothing to hide. They thought the Golden Flower shooter came to your apartment."

"I see..." Tera slowly nodded. *"I'm sorry that you had to lie to get me out."*

"I told no lie," Greta said, with a strong accent. *"You were lucky that forensics had all the data already collected. We have reason to believe that someone is tampering with evidence. Some collected items have gone missing."*

"What do you mean, you 'told no lie?'" Tera asked, a little confused.

"Don't worry, the truth always comes out in the end." The Inspector smiled. "And we were able to help prove that today. No State Policeman can make up a false story about you now."

Tera blinked a little, still unsure what to think. "But he was there…" she started. "The shooter did break into my apartment. I fought him. I cut his arm with my sword. He bled all over the floor. The sponge from my sink had to have been full of his DNA."

Greta looked a little worried.

"I don't know why you are saying this Tera, you don't have to protect yourself from me. We know the truth. No one was there that night." Greta handed Tera the file. "You can see it for yourself. The evidence is here. This was filed on Saturday afternoon."

Tera looked in disbelief at the data. The first thing she noticed was how long the list was. No fewer than seven separate swab samples were tested from her old apartment's kitchen floor, sword, and window. Then there was the gun, the glass, and all the other items they took. Even without the bloody sponge, they should have had a good case against her with those swab samples. The papers identified all traceable DNA as Tera's.

"But you altered this… right?"

Greta blinked slowly at Tera for a minute, trying to think of what she should say. Tera squinted at the file.

"He was actually there. The shooter was there..."

"Tera... sometimes when you experience something that is very hard to understand, like what happened at the restaurant, your mind plays tricks on you. You see things that are not real, and things can get confusing. But you don't need to explain anything to me. I understand your situation."

Inspector Greco spoke so eloquently, and while Tera could acknowledge a part of what she was hearing, there was an unsettling feeling growing inside of her.

"You know that no one was trying to hurt you on Sunday night? You were not attacked at your new apartment, Tera. You did that to yourself too."

Tera felt her body sink as the Inspector looked at her with pity in her eyes. Tera's skin began to feel clammy, and her sore legs began to start trembling. Panic, once again, was threatening to take over.

"Right, right... but I'm talking about before. At the old apartment. On Friday night, he actually was there."

Greta looked at her hands.

"I think you need some rest," she said. "You've been through so much these last few days. You need to take what time you have and rest."

"I'm the one who tampered with the evidence... I'm the one who took the sponge."

Greta looked at Tera, a little surprised.

"You? Tampered with the evidence? That's an interesting thing to say... But Tera, if that's true, then you know we are not missing a... sponge. We're missing the pills."

"Pills?"

They were approaching the Carabinieri Command Station. The Chief Inspector closed her eyes and continued.

"I probably shouldn't be telling you this now. I didn't realize that you actually believed... it would probably be best for us to protect you for a few more days before resuming the... plan." She took out her phone, now looking very worried.

Tera tried not to freak out. What was this woman saying? That night at the old apartment had to have been real. It had to have been.

"What about the phone call? The shooter called me. He left me a voicemail."

Greta looked at Tera. She spoke slowly and bothered.

"I wondered if you would bring that up. You are forgetting that we had your computer, Tera. We found the website that you use to forward your calls."

"I don't know what you're talking about..."

"Well Tera... we want to believe you, but what makes more sense? That the killer visited you of all people, left you unharmed, and ran away scared? From a musician?"

Tera looked blankly at the woman.

"Or that you bought a cheap cell phone and called yourself? Wanting to make your life more exciting. Hoping to find meaning and value in the drama. Trying to make... sense out of your personal traumatic history, by... making yourself the focus of a tragic scenario that you cannot... remove from your head. It was you, Tera. Nobody else was there. Not on Sunday. Not on Friday."

Greta casually waved her hands around the vehicle as she continued.

"The only value you are adding to this investigation is that you are succeeding in fooling the enemies as well as yourself. How long have you been taking those drugs? We found enough in your apartment to kill an elephant. You could easily be suffering from memory loss or hallucinations as a side effect of your addiction."

"My what?" Tera held her hands up near her face. The car started to spin. She couldn't focus on anything.

"Your counselor told us about your problem with substances. It's no wonder you have such a hard time sleeping at night. Your body is practically immune to your sleep medication. That's why you could survive over twenty milligrams of Versed and still wake up alive the next morning. And you can say what you want about not wanting to die, Tera. You knew what you were doing. You wanted to be missed. You wanted to be a true victim of your imaginary villain. Everyone would believe that the killer had come to you, to take you down because of your... great importance."

The car was parked inside the alcove of the large Command complex.

"Everyone wants to be important. I can understand that. But you need to wake up. There are people out there whose lives are in danger because of the lies you are telling.

We are wasting our efforts trying to protect you, and use you, and find out what is true and what is false. And that poor Sergeant… we asked him to keep an eye on you. We didn't think he would take things so far so fast." Greta looked at Tera in the eyes, annoyed. "You make this whole process so… so complicated."

The tiny woman opened her door and stepped out. She told the driver to hold, and started to talk on the phone. Tera felt so sick. So disoriented. She wondered if this was her kidnapping, and what sort of drug she had been given to feel so goddamn awful. She wasn't addicted to anything. She hadn't had sleep medication since she left the States. She never got her prescriptions renewed in Italy. Right?

Tera shakily unfastened her seatbelt, opened her door, and stumbled out of the car onto the concrete, promptly throwing up. Greta lowered her phone from her ear, gasping.

"*Prendi dell'acqua!*" She shouted at the driver, and rushed over to steady Tera, moments before she passed out.

31

"I want to go home." Tera was pale and disturbed.

"You won't be protected at home," Russo responded.

"I don't trust you. I don't feel safe here."

"Don't be absurd," Greta whispered, rolling her eyes.

"I don't believe your lies. I know what really happened. I don't want to do this anymore."

"You have two options, Tera. Either you comply with us and stay wired, or you stay here."

Tera thought about Fabrizia, telling her to "choose."

"Then let me go. I'll stay wired, just let me go. I don't want to be here anymore."

Worried looks were exchanged before Russo finally nodded. They escorted her back to the car, and dropped her off at her apartment.

She was having trouble unlocking that first door. There wasn't anything wrong with the key, she just kept dropping it, and fumbling while trying to turn it. She finally let another tenant help her.

"I must look crazy…" Tera thought. "Unable to unlock a door…" She thanked the kind fifty-something-year-old, and frantically moved down the hall to her room, humiliated, confused, and horribly anxious.

She paused outside the door to her unit, her whole body shaking. She closed her eyes and tried to breathe steadily. She thought about what the Inspector Chief had said. She thought about the pills. About the night she drugged herself. She tried to remember as much as she could about what really happened. It was true that Midazolam has a side effect of memory loss. It was possible that Tera forgot something. Could she have made up the story about the shooter in her old apartment, and then forgotten that it was only a lie?

She opened her door and looked in. It looked the same as yesterday. She walked inside and closed the door. She thought about the medication. If she was hiding pills in her apartment, where would she put them? Tera walked to the piano and opened the lid. She saw no drugs stashed away, but the blood money was gone too. She saw some paper sticking out of the lower strings, and hesitantly retrieved it. It was the check, from Carlos. She closed up the piano. She sat on her couch, afraid she might suddenly remember something horrible about herself. What happened on Sunday night? She could remember pretty well what she had planned to do, but did she actually end up doing it?

She remembered meeting with Carlos. She remembered cutting copies of her keys inside the local market. What did she do after that? How did she get the drugs? Tera stood up and walked over to her bedroom. She remembered Luca walking her home. He kissed her, and she freaked out. She definitely remembered that. Tera looked at her bed. She saw something on the floor in the back corner of the room. Her instincts told her that it was either a rat, or a large bug, so she immediately climbed onto her bed, and slowly approached it to learn how serious this was. It was a sock. A black sock. She got off her bed and picked it up. This was not her sock... was it?

She looked around the floor, trying to find its mate. For some reason, this was now incredibly important. She looked under the bed, and in her closet. She looked in her dresser. She looked back at her bed, pulled off the bedspread, and shook it out. She left the bedspread on the floor and climbed onto the bed, exploring under the top sheet. She found the other black sock. She sat up. It wasn't hard for her imagination to fill in the gaps. Luca didn't stay that night, did he?

Tera's mind was spinning in circles around itself as reality felt like a list of options before her. She grabbed a pencil and some nearby sheet music. It was hard enough to answer other people's questions, but questioning herself was proving to be the trickiest thing yet. She closed her eyes, took a deep breath, and decided to start from the beginning. The beginning being, with Carlos, on Sunday night, at the *osteria*.

She remembered leaving him there, while the sad guitarist tried to make sense out of the crummy sound system. She flipped over the sheet music and wrote that down. What did she do first after she left? She came home. Tera wrote that down. After she came home, she grabbed the prescription for her sleep medication. She walked to the pharmacy across the street. Tera wrote this down. She looked at the paper. She flipped it back over and walked to the piano.

This was page two of Maurice Ravel's Menuet. Ravel was a french impressionist composer, and Tera was very fond of his piano music. She rifled through her papers and put the whole piece together in front of her on the piano. This, THIS, was something that made perfect sense to her. She shook out her arms and began to play through the piece on that slightly detuned piano. She was playing it tenderly, from beginning to end, listening to the melody float above the harmonies in its pure, singable clarity. It carried such peace within it.

The colors of the notes together formed such lovely pictures in Tera's mind. She could easily see herself on a patio, looking out at a garden, lush green life all around her. It was raining, and some mysterious energy that excited her was moving slowly through the garden, drawing her in, showing her the best and most beautiful flowers. Her apartment still smelled of the fresh buttercups and larkspur that were sticking out of her boot-shaped vase on the table. Things started to feel fresher.

Life was beginning to grow in that space, inside the room, inside of her. The music now seemed to ask the kindest questions of Tera, as she played through it. And the answers all seemed obvious. They were all beauty, and wonder, and Tera found that even the hardest questions that this music could ask her had answers that were simple. She was so relaxed by the end of the piece, feeling that if this music could make sense of its own mysterious nature, then surely her mind could find rest. The song ended with Tera examining a small, tender flower within that dream of a garden. She remembered who she was. She was not her own, and she was not alone.

Thinking back to Sunday night, the part that Tera remembered the best was Luca walking her home. She specifically remembered when he asked her if she stole anything. She had just gone to six separate pharmacies and lied her face off about having a miscommunication with her counselor because of the language barrier between them. She showed them her old prescription and offered to pay cash for the inconvenience, spending the rest of the blood money. In this way, she was able to successfully convince all six pharmacies to give her the largest doses of liquid Midazolam permissible under Italian law, which wasn't much. But all together, she had about fifteen milligrams. She never had any pills. Greta was lying.

Tera stood up from the piano, resolute. The air felt clear, and she felt strong and confident. She began to think. If Greta was lying to her, then the chances were pretty good that she was lying to everyone. Greta was probably the corruption that the Carabinieri had suspected was within the State Police. But this was a big problem since Greta was intricately involved with everything the Carabinieri were doing. Tera remembered, with great worry, that it was Greta who issued the "cease and desist" notice to the State Police.

It was Greta who walked Tera out of the police station. It was Greta who oversaw the forensic evidence, the written testimonies, and the installment of Tera's tracking devices.

Tera grabbed her phone. She called "The Money." Her phone gave her an odd sound and dropped the call. This wasn't good. Tera tried to call Luca, but the results were the same. Tera entered her bathroom and pulled out her tweezers. She looked at the fingernail that contained the small tracer. The tweezers were not going to cut it. She took out one of the knives from under her slacks. Her hand began to shake, and she suddenly became aware of her foot pain. Maybe she was taking the wrong approach to this. She put the knife back and leaned against the wall, her palms were sweaty now. She looked into her mouth in the mirror, but she couldn't even find whatever it was they put on her tooth.

She tore the paper corner off of a musical score, and wrote down the phone number for "The Money." She grabbed her gun and thought about stuffing it down her shirt before tucking it into her pants. She felt so uncomfortable about that, but she wasn't taking any chances. She left her coat, sandals, and phone in the apartment, then knocked on her neighbor's door. No one answered, so she knocked on another door. She heard movement inside, but no one came to answer. Tera was beginning to wish she had never moved from her old apartment. She tried a third door, shouting in as she knocked.

"*Aiuto! Aiuto! Chiamate la polizia!*"

She could hear the neighbor inside yelling back,

"Leave us alone!"

Tera couldn't understand this at first, but then she remembered that the police had been here only two days ago, carrying her out on a stretcher. Whoever her neighbors were now, they were not what she was used to, and they truly *didn't* want to be involved. She knew she was only a twenty-minute walk from the Police Headquarters, so she figured she could borrow somebody's phone on the way there. And if not, she could just walk in and tell them herself. Two blocks out, she asked an older couple to borrow their phone and was able to call her number for Russo. But the phone was answered by Napolitano. The older couple watched with concerned faces as Tera yelled into the phone, not even giving the Lieutenant a chance to finish saying *"Dimmi."*

"Greta is lying! You have to stop her! She is the corruption!"

"Who is this?"

"It's Tera. Greta lied about…"

"Oh… Tera! Don't worry, we've got everything under control. But thank you for calling."

He hung up. That idiot hung up on her. She called back. The phone rang and rang. It never even went to voicemail. Tera thanked the perplexed couple and continued her trek to police headquarters, trying and failing to not confidence-check her gun every two minutes. She wasn't sure who she was more afraid of now: the Carabinieri, or the people who were supposed to kidnap her. She wanted

218

nothing more than to be locked back up in that State Police cell.

She made it halfway through the parking lot before she was recognized. She saw agent Romano inside speaking into his radio, looking at her with his hand on his gun. But things would be so different this time, because this time, Tera had a gun too. If they wouldn't listen to her, she could draw her weapon, and she was sure they would gladly drag her back into that cell. Assuming she didn't get shot first. She opened the door.

"I need to talk to Luca," she said in English, not thinking. *Agente* Romano made a strange face at her, while the agent behind the glass window seemed startled. Romano nodded slowly,

"The Sergeant is unavailable right now. You will have to wait."

She didn't want to wait. She refused to wait. She stared at him. He stared back.

"*Ho una pistola,*" she said slowly and started to lift her shirt and reach for it. Tera was really impressed with how fast this Scraggy guy was. She didn't even get to pull the gun out of her pants before he had her pinned to the floor. And he wasn't gentle with her this time either. He had a good face-to-floor smash going on. He cuffed her hands and pulled out her gun. It wasn't loaded. Typical Tera.

Romano and another policeman dragged Tera down the hallway to her cell; she happened to look at Luca's office door when they passed. What she saw took her breath away. She would have preferred to have been shot. Through the tinted glass window she could clearly make out the image of Luca with his arms around a young woman, their faces as close as Tera's had just been to the floor.

"That didn't take very long…" she said out loud, utterly flabbergasted, her heart slowly disintegrating within her. Romano and the other agent looked at her, clueless. Of all the confusing things she had experienced in the last twenty-four hours, this one seemed the most surreal. Had it all been a lie? Or had she been kidding herself this whole time? They never made it to the cell. Halfway down the last stretch of hallway, both of the men collapsed. Tera stood in place, cuffed and confused, looking at their bodies lying on the ground on both sides of her. She looked around her. There was no one in sight. She looked up at the security camera.

"I didn't do it!" she said, to the camera. Moments later she felt a small prick on her neck, and slowly watched the world around her turn into black spots, the sound of quick footsteps being the last thing she heard before she too collapsed.

32

Thursday.

She felt them push her into something solid, cold, and bulky. They shoved her down to the ground and zip-tied her hands together around what felt to her arms like wet, cold metal. They took the bag off of her head. She blinked and squinted, reacting to the lights. It was the man from the salon, kneeling over her. He had a bandage on his face. Looked like a broken nose. She got one good look at him before he hit her. He slapped her hard across the head. It shook her, but it wasn't the worst she'd been hit. The other man didn't look familiar, but he didn't look friendly. Tera felt tired, hungry, and dehydrated; her tongue was drying out as the gag in her mouth collected all of her spit.

"*Brava stronzina!*" The man with the broken nose grabbed her face by the jaw.

"You think you're so clever, running away. I hope she lets me crush you."

He threw her face harshly to the side before standing up. The two men spoke to each other in some dialect that Tera couldn't follow, occasionally laughing in a horrible way. Before long, an old metal door opened, and a slim woman in black leather streamed in. She looked fierce, like an actress from one of those Italian soaps. Her hair was long, flowing past her shoulders, wavy and black. Her lips were red, and her eyes were like daggers. She had a small thin nose and a dimple in her chin. She had a face that told you everything and nothing. She was truly stunning.

"Thank you, boys. That will be all for now." She took off her gloves and threw them at Tera.

"Ciao Tera," the lady in black said, while the two men left through the old metal door.

"Or should I call you... Iris?"

Tera didn't feel great about this. She would have said, "my name's not Iris, you frickin' lunatic," but she still had a gag in her mouth.

"You've been fun to watch..." the lady in black continued, *"and what a confusing web we had to get through just to bring you here. But don't worry. Our friend should be here soon."* She looked to the side, with what looked like desire in her eyes. *"I've never met a man like him before. Have you? Impenetrable. Intrepid. I hope he treated you better than I treated him. He's going to pay for his mistakes with his life."* She looked at Tera with curious eyes.

"Oh, I can't help myself. I have to know." She took a switchblade from her belt and cut off Tera's gag. Tera stretched her face, as the pinched nerves and muscles relaxed back into place. The woman kept the switchblade uncomfortably close to Tera's face.

"What did he break first? Your window, or your heart? You loyal little rodent, scurrying around the police like a clueless idiot. That must have been fun for you, trying to win him back with your little games. But he never came back for you, did he?"

Tera gathered what moisture in her mouth was left, spitting the fuzzes out.

"You suck." She stared back into the woman's eyes, angry and crushed.

"Oh Iris, you don't look very happy. What's the matter?" The woman smiled at her, greatly amused.

Tera thought about how to answer. Did she want to try to play this out? To be Iris? Whoever that was supposed to be? Maybe it was the chemicals in her system, or the emotional exhaustion that led her to blurt out the truth.

"My boyfriend is cheating on me."

"Boyfriend?" It was Luca. He was apparently in the room too, somewhere behind her.

"Are you referring to me?"

Tera's eyes stretched wide open with fury.

"You traitor! You good for nothing, double-timing jerk! You swine-faced pig-police hog!"

"Hey, hey, hey! *Posso spiegare!*" He tried to speak over her.

"Explain?! How the hell are you going to explain that!? I saw you in your office with your hands all over her body!"

"Yeah, yeah, well... she..." he paused slightly, "she is my wife."

Teras eyes raged further, strong energy moved her dramatically from side to side in front of that large metal pipe. Her mouth gaping wide in shock.

"Your w...wife?!" she screamed out. "You're a... horrible husband!" she stuttered in anger. *"Wear a damn wedding ring you son of a dog! That poor woman!"*

The lady in black chimed in, slightly amused.

"Oh, she isn't poor."

Tera looked up at the diva in front of her. For a second, she had forgotten that she was there. Tera squinted at her and thought quickly.

"Oh..." she coughed, beginning to understand. "SHE... is your wife." Tera could remember now, the woman in the office had that same wavy, black hair.

"Come now, you can do better than him. He hardly remembers how to undress a woman." She gave Tera a horrible smile. The lights in the room flickered out. The humming of nearby equipment went silent. Tera hadn't even noticed the loud machine sounds, but now that they had stopped, the room felt like it had negative sound flushing through it. Her heart and her breathing seemed unbearably loud. Her head was pounding.

The only light entering that room was through a small foggy window at the top of that metal door. The woman in black walked toward that light.

"Unlike someone I know. Looks like it's showtime." She pushed her way through the door, which closed with a clang behind her. Tera remained seated in the darkness.

33

"So…" Tera started, "are you evil too? Are you going to kill me now?" She heard some shifts from behind her.

"No," Luca said, bothered. "I am also tied up."

"Ok." She tried to swallow. They sat in silence. There were so many things to process. Tera was still trying to determine where they were and how to get out. This crazy chick in black leather seemed interesting enough, but she couldn't wrap her head around the idea that she was Luca's wife. Or that Luca was there. Or that Luca was a married man.

"So what the hell?!" she called into the darkness. Luca gave a frustrated sigh.

"I didn't think you'd care."

"That you're married?!"

"Why would you care, Tera? Or is your name Iris?"

"I'm not… I'm not Iris! Who is Iris? Iris was just that stupid song he wanted me to play for his… screwed up… crime scene exit music…"

"How long have you been working with that spy? How long was Garbanzo siphoning off drug money for The Blind Man?"

"Wha… what? Who is… the Blind Man? Garbanzo is dead, right? I saw him get shot! I'm not working for anybody, Luca! My boss was Riccardo Di Maggio, and he was killed a week ago."

Luca went silent, deep in thought.

"Why did your wife tie you up, huh? What's that about?"

"It's a very long story."

"Well…" Tera responded, "I think we've got some time."

"Ok, you start," Luca snapped back. "Why did she call you Iris?"

Tera thought about it.

"I think she thinks I'm Greta."

"Greta?" Luca said softly.

"Inspector Greta Greco… was lying… had me thinking I was insane. She manipulated forensic evidence to make me look innocent. Well, not that I'm guilty, but, that's not the point. The Carabinieri closed the case for the State Police because they suspected a traitor. But I think the traitor was Greta. She's probably Iris, if there is an actual person named Iris."

"Why did you lie about the shooter?" he asked calmly.

"Because that monster who just hit me in the head was threatening me and my friends. Because he was working for your wife!"

"Why were you at the station during the attack?"

"I was trying to get help!"

"What other lies did you tell me?" He sounded less upset.

"I never lied to you, Luca. Not once." Tera started to calm down. "I lied to some pharmacists... I lied a few times... to myself... But I never lied to you."

The darkness in the room was slowly starting to lighten up as Tera's eyes adjusted to it. She could hear Luca breathing.

"Ok," he finally said, sounding discouraged. "Ok."

"Your turn." Tera was still unsure what to think. "Why are you here?"

"My guess is that I am going to be ransomed. Or framed for Russo's death. Or maybe she wants to kill me here. I'm not exactly sure... *Ohimè.*"

"Russo is dead?" Tera couldn't believe it.

"He was killed last night, during the attack at headquarters. Kalypso shot him with his own gun."

"Who is Kalypso?" She waited.

"That wicked woman who was just here." After a deep sigh, he changed his tone. "If it wasn't for you, she would have shot me with my own gun too. You taught me a valuable lesson the other day. I thank you for that."

"What happened at headquarters?"

"They cleaned us out. At least three agents are dead, maybe more. They took out our power, knocked out our security. It makes a lot more sense since you mentioned Greta. It had to have been an inside job."

"Why? Why would they do this?"

"To stop the investigation. To send a message to law enforcement in Apulia. Kalypso certainly wanted me dead, and it seems she is deeply involved in some political scheme."

Tera's heart sank to think that more people were now dead. She tried to stay focussed.

"So what's up with you and her?"

Luca mumbled a few things that Tera didn't catch... maybe calling her a "siren" or something like that.

"I met that witch when I was in the Air Force. We had a love affair... It was foolish. I thought I was in love with her... no... it's true. I was. She was so outrageous and alluring, I was... I was crazy about her. We were together for two or three years, and..." he took a breath, *"we were eventually married when I was twenty-four. We had to wait because she was... much younger than me."*

Luca sounded ashamed recounting all of this. Tera leaned her head back against the pipe and listened on.

"And it was... it was a hard relationship to manage. Shortly after we were married, she told me she was pregnant. I was so... happy, so excited to be a father. But after a few months, she told me that the child was not mine. She left me for a businessman in Rome. I was... greatly devastated."

Tera could tell that it was very difficult for him to talk about this. He sounded defeated.

"But after a few months, she found me again. The man for which she had left me wanted to marry her, but couldn't unless we were divorced. You have to understand, Tera. In Italy, divorce takes a very long time. She filed first. He was paying for it. I didn't want to give her

up. I wanted to make it work. I was willing to push my entire family away to make it work."

Tera listened intently, waiting for him to continue.

"I was an idiot."

Outside the door, a booming, distant explosion rattled the environment. The two of them waited, but nothing happened.

"When two people in Italy want to divorce, it's three years if both parties agree, but five if they don't. But after only one and a half years, he gave up on her, threw her out, keeping their child. She was ruined. She came back to me with nothing, and I was a fool. I took her back. We stopped the divorce proceedings. I thought that I could make it work. She stayed with me for a few weeks, and it seemed like we would finally be together. One day, I came home from work, and she was gone. She had stolen more than half of my money, and run. I didn't hear a word from her for another five months, until she again wanted a divorce. Now she wanted to marry a politician in Sicily.

I hated her, Tera. I hated her. I wanted nothing more than to make her suffer. Again, I refused to sign, I wanted her to wait and pay for the full five years. And she gave me hell for that. Absolute hell. But those five years will be completed this October. Until then, she is still my wife."

Luca took a moment before he went on.

"After everything that happened with her, my heart had no part remaining that Kalypso hadn't eviscerated. I trusted no one with my love. I didn't think I ever would again. But time passed. The legal proceedings took place in the shadows, and eventually, and slowly, my heart began to heal. And then," his voice started to indicate a smile,

"I met this beautiful young woman. She was foreign, and deeply captivating. The more I learned about her, the more I felt a connection. The more I wanted to know her. I felt my heart beat again. It was like the glorious sun rising after a very long night of darkness. My joy was returning to me, and for a few days, it was like Kalypso had never existed."

Tera said nothing.

"But on Sunday, that world evaporated... the very devil called me, told me she was at the train station in Foggia."

Luca kicked the edge of the floor with his shoe. *"Told me she was... coming home for good. I told her to go to hell, but she... she has this way to twist your mind, cause you to forget. I offered her five thousand Euros to leave. She said she didn't want my money. She said she wanted me."*

He laughed.

"I didn't believe that. How could I believe that. She is such a... lying temptress. She waved my name around the whole city, gaining access to my apartment, my connections, my work..." he swallowed.

"As for cheating on you..." Luca sounded a bit nervous.

"I wish I could tell you that I was... using her, or something, but I... I hate her. I hate her, Tera. I am greatly sorry."

The room was filled with silence. After an uncomfortable amount of time, Luca started to feel concerned.

"Tera?"

"Yeah," she responded immediately. There was another long stretch of silence.

"I thought my marriage had a horrible ending. But that…" she shook her head and sighed. She didn't know how to respond to something like this. She tried to pull herself up, to lean her shoulders more comfortably against the bulky metal knobs.

"What was he like?" Luca asked, gently.

"Who?" Tera asked.

"Your husband. What was he like?"

"Oh... Max?" Tera's world exploded with memories when she heard herself say his name. It had been a long time since she said his name. She felt a deep sadness well up inside her. Her tired body proved its resilience by still producing tears somehow. Flashes of the past swept over her. Simple things, like Max holding her hand. Their first kiss. The time they got the van stuck in the snow. The fights they had over money and work. The vacation trip they took to Texas. She remembered sitting in the bar the night they met. He was playing his guitar, singing a song she had never heard before. She said he was the only man in that town with talent.

"Oh, Max…" she cried, leaning forward, to keep her back from banging into the metal pipes as her chest heaved. Tera could hear Luca fidgeting slightly with his own set of pipes behind him. He wanted to hold her, but his hands were bound, and he couldn't even turn his head far enough to see her. Tera breathed as she was able.

"He was… spontaneous," Tera recalled, quietly, between sobs.

"He would get us in the car, and just drive. I never knew where we would go until we got there. He… he built houses. And wrote songs. We were a pretty good duet, you know, but he was better than me." She laughed. "He worked so hard, and loved me so well." She felt the tears roll down her face.

"Those were the... best years of my life."

Luca waited.

"Tera… how did you do it? How did you forgive the man who killed him?"

She sniffed a few times and coughed a little. She spoke slowly.

"I... I like the way you put it, the other day. You said that perfect love is stronger than fear. Well, love is stronger than hate, too."

"I don't think I could ever forgive her."

"Yeah… you probably can't. Not if you're trying to use your own love to forgive. Nobody's perfect, Luca."

34

There was another distant boom.

"I'd like to get us out of here…" Luca said, after a moment. "Do you have any ideas?"

"Well…" Tera squeaked, "I do have some knives strapped to my legs."

"What?" he startled, excitedly.

"Yeah, they're just kind of hard to reach. Um…" Tera tried to get her legs beneath her, to see if she could push herself up to standing. The pipe curved sharply behind her, running sideways into a concrete wall, near an opening. Luca was on the other side of that wall. Unable to go up, she let herself slump down, onto her side, her face now pressing against the cold, dirty floor. It smelled like mold and rust; felt like rough pavement against her cheek. She kicked her legs around to the opening.

"Are your legs bound?" she called over.

"No." He pulled his arms against the pipe, trying to make it budge. It was solid, and stronger than he was.

"Can you reach my legs with yours?"

"Ah…" Luca liked this idea. Tera could hear him kick off his shoes. He slid himself along the pipe, getting his back as close to the wall as he could, turning and bending his knees, he felt his foot hit Tera's leg.

"Hi there…" he laughed. "Which leg has the knives?"

"Hang on…" Tera pulled her legs back up to her, and wiggled uncomfortably, trying to slide her pants off. They were a little big on her anyway, so she was able to slowly inch them down, her bare skin scraping against the floor. It was cold, and rough, and it stung. She felt her right thigh get cut on some small sharp thing that was poking out of the floor. She cried out in pain.

"Tera?"

"I'm ok…" She struggled on. She got her pants to slide down further, just to the top of the higher knife.

"Ok, so…" She felt weird about this, but she didn't have to try to explain her idea. Luca was already on it. He slid his foot carefully up the outside of her left leg, until his toes felt the gauze under her slacks. She winced in pain, and he quickly pulled back his foot.

"It's higher…" she mumbled. He stretched his leg as far as he could reach, just barely touching the hilt of the knife with his toes.

"What do you think?" Tera asked. "Can you get it?"

"I think so…" he said, hopefully, "eventually…"

He tried tugging on the hilt with his toes, but it was slippery. He tried switching his feet, but it was equally as difficult on this side. After an exasperated sigh, he tried using both feet together. He tried this for several minutes with no success before he finally gave it a rest. Tera waited, wondering what else they could try to use.

"Did you really spit on a judge?" he asked lightly.

"No... that was a joke. Sorry." She tried to smile amidst her discomfort and worry.

"If we make it out of here alive," Luca said, "you will have to remember me to introduce you to my mother."

It took Tera a second to figure out what Luca meant. But yes, she thought, she could remind him to do that.

Luca took a moment to rethink their situation before he changed his approach. He brought his foot down lower, towards Tera's knee, and gently pushed up on the tip of the knife blade, to push it out from the bottom.

"Careful..." she whispered.

He gently kicked at the knife, until it jumped out onto the floor with a beautiful sound of metal on stone. They both sighed in relief, laughing a bit with the sense of accomplishment. Tera carefully moved her legs and pushed the knife along the floor with her foot, down towards Luca. He slowly used his feet to get the knife to his hands. Cutting the zip tie took about five seconds. Luca scrambled across the dirty floor, and cut Tera free. Kneeling, he helped her up into his arms. They held onto each other on the floor in that dark room for a short while, worn and pained, just breathing together. Within his warm arms, Tera could feel that Luca wasn't wearing a police vest. Any shots coming his way would hit his body. He had no gun, no phone, no radio.

"It's not over yet," Luca said. "Can you stand?"

Tera took a minute to redress herself and Luca grabbed his shoes and dirty white socks. She rewrapped the smaller knife to the outside of her pants, letting Luca keep the larger blade. He helped her up, and together they walked slowly to the door.

In the light from the window, they could now see how terrible they looked. Tera's face had dirt smeared all over one side, up into her short greasy hair, and her ear was bleeding down her neck. She had red eyes from crying, and looked completely wiped out. Luca's white shirt and arms were covered in dirt from the floor. Apart from that, he actually looked pretty good. Just tired and upset.

Luca went first. He opened the door, knife in hand, and looked out into the bright, large hanger. There was no one in sight at first, until he spotted four bodies on the ground in the distance. The large door to the hanger was open. It was a sunny day. Near the outside of the utility room, which they were now leaving, there was a tall row of crates. Luca looked around the corner, then led Tera out into the hanger with him. They rounded the corner and stood behind the crates.

"Stay here…" he said, and carefully made his way over to the bodies on the ground. He kept his eyes peeled for motion, making his way closer. He saw what he was hoping for. Next to the first man down was a loaded pistol. He ran to the bodies and grabbed the gun, cocked it, and retreated to the row of crates. Tera watched in awe and admiration as Luca moved. He was quick and methodical. She was glad she was on his side.

A helicopter could be heard in the distance. Tera wondered if that was help coming their way. An arm came around Tera's neck, and pulled her back, a hand covering her mouth before she could scream. The man with the broken nose lifted Tera a few inches into the air - her legs kicking - and started to carry her to the side of the hanger.

"I was just on my way for you..." The words seeped from the man's mouth like a death sentence. Tera grabbed her knife and stabbed the man in the leg. He cried out and loosened his grip, and Tera fell forward to the ground, leaving the knife in his leg. She turned around on her elbows to see him drawing his gun. Time slowed down as she watched him pull the Swiss pistol out of his pocket. Frozen, she looked helplessly up from the ground as he pulled the slide, loading a bullet into the chamber. She couldn't make herself move, and in this moment felt resigned to her final breath.

He aimed the gun at her - the same gun that he threatened her with all those days ago. Tera heard two loud shots, and watched the man stagger and fall backward, reacting to the two bullets that hit him in the chest. Luca rushed over to the man and took his gun. He helped Tera up and handed her the fallen man's forty-five. Together they ran to the hanger's entrance.

35

From the large mouth of the hanger they could see the remains of a helicopter, not far off: a smoldering twist of metal, smoking up to the sky. There were two more bodies on the ground in the other direction. The sound of a helicopter in flight grew louder. In the distance they could see coastline; steep cliffs breaking off sharply down to the crashing shore.

"Drop your weapons!"

The voice came from behind them. They both recognized it immediately.

"*Tenente?*" Luca shouted back, dropping the gun and raising his hands.

"*Conti! Santo cielo...*" The Lieutenant lowered his gun, the other law enforcement with him followed suit. Napolitano had roughly thirty men with him, slowly working their way into the building from the opposite side.

"Cociarelli thought you were dead!" the Lieutenant yelled over.

"I've never been so happy to hear your voice," Luca smirked as he turned around. "*Uniamoci!*"

"*Sì, sì...*" Napolitano shouted back and smiled. *"Let us join in cohort! Conti, is that woman still alive?"*

"This one is," Luca motioned to Tera. She turned around slowly and held onto the Swiss pistol.

"I owe you an apology, Signorina," Napolitano called over. "You were correct about the Chief Inspector."

Tera nodded. They had hardly had time to lower their guard before gunshots rang out from deep within the hanger. The Italian law enforcement team flew into action, whipping around and fighting back in glorious form. It was a beautiful picture of elite training and teamwork as the men in black uniforms advanced through the hanger, their backs reading either "Polizia" or "Carabinieri" in white letters. Most of the opposition was apprehended alive as the agents systematically moved through their lines, like a choreographed dance. Luca and Tera stayed put, taking cover outside of the large doorway.

One frenzied man came running out of the building with a gun in his hand, craning his neck to look behind him. Even with his back facing them, Tera recognized him as the unfriendly looking man from the utility room. The man was raising his gun, aiming at the Lieutenant, unaware inside. Luca charged at him and wrestled him for the gun. Tera watched the struggle, unsure of what to do. She looked at the gun in her hands and called for help from the police inside. They were busy. She looked back at Luca. He had the man's gun in a stable grip, but the man was slowly turning the gun towards Luca.

"Take the shot!" he yelled to Tera. Her aim wasn't that reliable. She couldn't risk it.

"No!" she shouted back.

"Tera! Take the shot! Take the shot!" The unfriendly man was winning the struggle for the gun. Tera aimed low. Her shot hit its mark, but not without knocking Luca to the ground as well. The unfriendly man dropped the gun and cried out in pain, holding his side.

"Luca!" Tera ran to the Sergeant. He was confused, and hadn't yet realized that he had also been shot. Tera kicked the other man's gun towards a Carabiniere in the hanger, who promptly made his way over to take care of the other man.

"I'll never forgive myself..." Tera leaned over Luca's body. His white shirt was spattered with red. She examined the wound on his arm, which was now starting to bleed profusely. She quickly rolled up her left pant leg and unwrapped some of the gauze from her knee, using it to bind up his wound. He sat up slowly,

"I'm ok, I'm ok, it just grazed me..."

"Oh, Luca... I'm so sorry! What have I done..."

He tried to calm her down, but she was convinced she had killed him. She took his head in her hands and kissed him, long and true. She looked at his face, and he blinked at her in awe.

"Shoot me again..." he whispered.

They found Kalypso Conti, unconscious, next to her dead lover - Senator Montefusco, also known as "The Blind Man." Her dreams of being the Prime Minister's wife were as broken as her late lover's corrupt political vision. Her crimes would hold her in prison until the day she died. They never found Greta Greco. She managed to erase herself from the grid, leaving no trace of her presence before disappearing back into the system from which she and her kind emerge. As for the British spy, Tera swears she saw him hitch a ride on a small sailing vessel off the coast of the Adriatic Sea, but no one could really be sure.

A line of police vehicles took off, sirens wailing away. Inside the Carabinieri's Fiat Ducato, Tera lay her head against Luca's chest, listening to his heartbeat. He held her in his arms until she fell safely asleep. Tera did manage to get her key back from Luca once they reached Foggia. She stayed in that new apartment of hers until Luca gave her the key to his, after a ceremony - late, on a Saturday; in October, in America.

Made in the USA
Monee, IL
26 February 2022

91930060R00142